CAROLE MORTIMER

undying love

Harlequin Books

TORONTO • NEW YORK • LONDON
AMSTERDAM • PARIS • SYDNEY • HAMBURG
STOCKHOLM • ATHENS • TOKYO • MILAN

For
John and Matthew

Harlequin Presents first edition November 1983
ISBN 0-373-10645-9

Original hardcover edition published in 1983
by Mills & Boon Limited

Printed in U.S.A.

"I was trying to ask you to marry me."

Marriage. It wasn't a word she had even thought of in connection with Rick.

"Shanna?" He sounded anxious when she didn't answer him. "Honey, this wasn't the way I had it planned—just blurting it out like this—but I love you, and I want to marry you. I don't like the impression your brother has of our relationship. I don't like anyone thinking that of you, but at the time it was all you would accept. Honey, please answer me, will you marry me?"

Shanna swallowed hard at the ragged pain in his voice, wishing with all her heart she could throw herself in his arms and never have to leave.

"I can't." She turned away. "I can't, Rick!"

Books by Carole Mortimer

Harlequin Presents

These books may be available at your local bookseller.

For a free catalog listing all titles currently available,
send your name and address to:

Harlequin Reader Service
2504 West Southern Avenue, Tempe, AZ 85282
Canadian address: Stratford, Ontario N5A 6W2

CHAPTER ONE

THE first person Shanna saw when she entered her brother's spacious lounge was Rick Dalmont. And that was enough to make her want to leave again!

But she met that black-eyed gaze without blinking, nodding cool acknowledgment before turning to talk to her sister-in-law, Janice. But she knew those strange dark eyes still watched her, was always aware of Rick Dalmont's gaze on her whenever they happened to meet. And that had been all too often lately as far as she was concerned.

'I'm so glad you made it,' Janice said with some relief; she was a small blonde-haired woman, married to Shanna's brother Henry for the last ten years; their two offspring, a boy and a girl, were fast asleep upstairs.

Shanna didn't need to question her sister-in-law's feeling of relief; she knew the reason for it—Rick Dalmont. Half Spanish, half American, the black-haired, black-eyed business tycoon had made no secret of his pursuit from the moment they met two weeks ago. Until that time a young up-and-coming actress had shared his life; she had been asked to leave the night Rick met Shanna for the first time. A lot of women would have been flattered by the almost single-minded pursuit by such a man—Rick Dalmont was a very eligible bachelor—but Shanna would rather he turned his attention elsewhere. Ricardo Dalmont, to give him his full name, wasn't her type at all. His reputation with women was no secret, his method of ending those relationships was not always gentle. In fact, it was very often cruel; the women were simply replaced, without notice.

7

But that wasn't the reason for Shanna's lack of interest; she simply wasn't interested in any man at the moment. Clinically she could admire Rick Dalmont's looks, the over-long black hair, the hard tanned face, the jet-black eyes that revealed none of the man's thoughts; his mouth was a cynical twist, his tall body leanly muscled, his sexual magnetism tangible even to the immune Shanna. But as a person she disliked him intensely, disliked all that he stood for.

'For goodness' sake get him away from Henry,' Janice pleaded with her. 'This is supposed to be a party, not a business meeting,' she groaned.

'I'm sure Henry doesn't mind,' Shanna said dryly, knowing her brother's preoccupation with business. She hadn't reached the age of twenty-five without learning that of her older brother.

'He probably introduced the subject,' the other woman nodded. 'But he suddenly seems to have lost Rick's attention,' she mocked dryly.

Shanna followed Janice's amused gaze, her green eyes clashing with his black ones. She had never seen eyes like Rick Dalmont's before, so dark a brown they appeared black. That dark gaze moved slowly over her body, from the smoothness of her straight shoulder-length black hair with the feathered fringe from a centre parting, her green eyes surrounded by dark sooty lashes, the small straight nose, the bright lip-gloss on her slightly pouting lips, the slenderness of her throat, the perfection of her body in the clinging knee-length red dress, her long legs thrust into black high-heeled sandals, adding to her already considerable height.

She met that intimate gaze with a challenge of her own, and made herself return the inventory, the over-long black hair swept back from the wide intelligent forehead, the harsh features carved as if from stone, the animal elegance of the powerful body beneath the black evening suit, the material stretched over wide shoulders, tapering to a narrow waist and powerful thighs. Rick Dalmont was a magnificent specimen of manhood; and he left Shanna cold, both physically and emotionally.

And he knew it too, had known of her coldness from the beginning, and it only increased his desire for her. She should have known such a man would consider her a challenge, that he would meet that challenge head-on. If she had known of his presence here, at what was primarily a private party for a few friends of her brother's, she would have refused the invitation. That was probably the reason Henry had remained silent; her brother was well aware of her feelings in regard to his new business acquaintance.

The newness of Henry's apparent friendship with the other man bothered her somewhat. Rick Dalmont wasn't a man's man; his relationships were mainly sensual, his many business interests seeming to be his only other occupation. The Dalmont fortune had been made by Todd Dalmont, Rick's father, originally in oil, but since Rick Dalmont had taken over fifteen years ago he had diversified the family fortune, successfully, into a number of different industries. A man like Rick Dalmont would be successful at anything he set out to do, from winning the woman of his choice to getting the best deal for Dalmont Industries!

And that was what bothered her. Henry and Rick had absolutely nothing in common socially. Henry was a staid family man, very much in love with his wife, whereas Rick Dalmont had made his opinion of marriage known on more than one occasion; he approved of it for other people, but not for himself. So that only left business that Henry could have in common with the other man, and yet even that didn't seem plausible, for as far as Shanna knew Rick Dalmont had no interest in the newspaper business, and as Henry ran and owned one of England's biggest newspapers . . .

'He's coming over,' Janice whispered softly.

She had been expecting it, could sense his presence even now, was aware of the warmth of his body as he came to stand beside her, could smell the spicy aftershave that was exclusive to him, as were the cheroots he smoked.

'Shanna,' he greeted in a voice of gravel and honey. She had been surprised by that voice the first time she heard it, had never heard such a smoothly seductive voice cloaked in such husky tones, his accent softly American.

'Mr Dalmont,' she returned smoothly, knowing he found her distant behaviour amusing.

'Could I get you a drink?' he offered gruffly.

'I'm sure Henry——'

'Rick knows the way to the bar,' her brother dismissed unhelpfully.

Shanna gave a haughty inclination of her head, left with no other choice. 'Then I accept your kind offer, Mr Dalmont.'

Her arm was taken between vicelike fingers as she was steered away from Henry and Janice and through to the bar in the adjoining room. 'I wasn't being kind at all, Shanna,' Rick told her softly. 'Not unless you count to myself. You left Doug Gillies' party two evenings ago before I even had the chance to talk to you.'

She would have left this evening too if it hadn't been her brother's party. 'I'm sorry,' she said coolly, only reaching up to his shoulder despite her own considerable height.

He grinned, deep grooves in the hardness of his cheek, his eyes a deep enigmatic black. 'You aren't sorry at all,' he derided. 'But I'll let it pass for now. Dry Martini, isn't it?' he nodded towards the bar.

Shanna didn't question his knowing her preference in drinks; this man would make it his business to find out her preferences in everything! 'Thank you,' she accepted distantly.

'My pleasure,' he drawled suggestively.

Shanna ignored the innuendo, realising that this man was used to a more positive reaction from women, that her indifference to him intrigued him. She had had no choice; she either showed him her indifference or gave him what he wanted. And as he wanted her, made no secret of the fact, she had decided to show him indifference. Either way he was sure to lose interest soon, and this way there was no harm to her. She had no intention of sleeping with a man just as a means of getting him out of her life! Rick Dalmont wasn't a man who enjoyed the chase for long, she just hoped he would tire of her soon; he was making it awkward for her to go anywhere, always seeming to be where she was.

'Here,' he held the long glass out to her, somehow managing to touch her slender fingers in the process. 'Not very subtle,' he acknowledged the slight raise of her brows. 'But I figured it's the only way to touch you at all. Do you usually freeze men off the way you've been freezing me?'

He was beginning to tire, she could tell that. Until tonight Rick Dalmont had shown her his attraction to her, but it had always been charmingly done, never a word or movement out of place. Tonight his behaviour was noticeably different; the chase was over, the feline abobout to catch his prey, any way he could. It was the time she had been dreading the most; her own polite but distant behaviour was no longer enough to repel him. She would have to be as blunt as he intended being.

She met his gaze unflinchingly, her black hair swinging back over her shoulders. 'Yes,' she answered abruptly.

The charm had gone from his face now, leaving his expression harsh, his mouth taut, his eyes narrowed. 'So I'm not the exception?' he bit out, seemingly unaware—or just unconcerned—of the people standing near them, the conversation and loud laughter doing a lot to mask this very private conversation.

'No,' she drawled, knowing the idea displeased him. Rick Dalmont was a man who arrogantly dismissed women when they displeased him; he was *never* dismissed himself. It would have been that way all his life; the Dalmont fortune had been made long before Todd took his young Spanish bride and produced Ricardo. Rick Dalmont had grown up with a gold spoon in his mouth, and the determined line of his mouth said he wasn't going to allow a mere woman to deny him something he wanted—even if it was her! For thirty-seven years nothing had been denied him, and Shanna Logan wasn't about to be the exception, not even when it was her body he wanted. 'What do you and my brother have to talk about so earnestly?' She decided attack was still the better form of defence.

Rick's mouth twisted derisively. 'He hasn't told you yet?'

'No,' she evaded.

'I wonder why?' he taunted.

She gave a careless shrug. 'I have no doubt he will, in time.'

Rick gave a haughty inclination of his head. 'In time. But will that be too late?'

'I have no idea. Will it?'

He gave a husky laugh. 'It could be,' he mocked her attempt to get information out of him.

'Then perhaps I'd better go and talk to Henry now.' She turned to leave.

Firm fingers grasped her arm, strong relentless fingers that held Shanna to his side. 'It can wait,' he dismissed abruptly. 'Maybe if you ask me nicely enough I might be persuaded to tell you.'

She eyed him coldly. 'I can get the information from Henry with much less effort.'

His breath was warm against her cheek. 'Would it be so much of an effort?'

'Yes!' she snapped—and then cursed herself for her show of anger. She had intended to show this man no emotion at all, but his manhandling of her couldn't go without retaliation of some sort. She pulled pointedly out of his grasp, knowing her arm was going to be bruised in the morning from his reluctance to release her. 'Yes, I'm afraid it would, Mr Dalmont,' she repeated coldly. 'And I hate having to make an effort of any kind.'

'Poor little rich girl,' he rasped.

Her cool green eyes openly mocked him. 'Isn't that slightly ridiculous, coming from you?'

'I worked for my place as head of Dalmont Industries from the time I could understand what stocks and shares were,' he bit out fiercely. 'My father never gave anyone anything for nothing in his life, and he wasn't about to start with me. What's your excuse?'

She had hit a raw nerve, she could tell that; Rick Dalmont would lose his temper only rarely. He had just done so very effectively. 'I don't have one,' she told him quietly. 'I'm the editor of a magazine Henry owns.'

'So he informed me,' Rick nodded abruptly. 'A cursory title, I'm sure.'

'Then don't be,' she snapped. '*Fashion Lady* may only be a women's magazine, and unimportant to a man like you, but I run it to the best of my ability.'

'And how good is that?'

She flushed at the quietly intended insult. 'Ask Henry!' her eyes flashed.

To her chagrin Rick Dalmont began to smile. 'At least this is an improvement. I've made you lose your temper with me three times in the last five minutes.'

'I think that probably makes us even,' she taunted.

'Nothing like it,' he still smiled. 'My temper has been much less controlled since I met you. But you could soon change that,' he added throatily. 'All it would take is one word from you.'

And she knew exactly what that word was! 'I haven't been using that word too often lately,' she said abruptly.

'Since your husband died.'

Shanna froze. 'What do you know about that?'

Rick shrugged. 'It's no secret that he died, is it?'

'No.' She avoided that black-eyed gaze, knowing this man could see into her soul if he wanted to. And from what she knew of him he would want to.

'Or how he died?' His eyes were narrowed now, sensing her increased hostility.

She swallowed hard. 'No.'

It had been no secret how Perry died, it had been emblazoned across the front page of every newspaper in the world. A famous ex-racing driver killed in a road accident was world-wide news.

'Or that you were in the car with him at the time?' Rick continued his prodding into her personal pain.

This time she didn't even answer him; her expression was wooden, refusing to show any emotion to this man. He would take any sign of weakness and use it to his advantage.

'Or that your marriage had already ended.'

The cruelly stated words brought a light sheen of perspiration to her brow, although her dull gaze remained fixed on one of the light-fittings on the far wall.

'That the two of you be together at all was an unusual occurrence.'

Her gaze slowly moved back to the hard face of the man standing in front of her, missing the taut enquiry of his expression, seeing only the determined cruelty of his eyes and mouth. 'If you'll excuse me, Mr Dalmont——'

'And if I won't?' Once again his fingers bruised her arm, but this time she didn't even feel the pain.

'You will.' The cold dullness of her voice made his hand drop away, and without another glance in his direction she walked away.

People rarely spoke to her of Perry, most of them respecting the fact that she must still feel her husband's loss after only six months. But Rick Dalmont had a hard cruelty about him that didn't respect anything, even a widow's grief. He had even mentioned the reports in some newspapers that her marriage to Perry had been far from happy at the end. Only an insensitive swine could have done that. Rick Dalmont would use anything to get what he wanted, including her grief for Perry.

'Shanna,' Henry touched her arm lightly. 'What have you said to Rick?' he asked anxiously. 'He looks like thunder.'

She blinked up at her brother, her elder by five years, his receding hairline adding to his air of maturity. Although right now he looked very worried.

'You haven't upset him, have you?' He kept shooting worried glances at the other man.

'Does it look like it?' she mocked. Rick Dalmont was

now leaning against the wall talking softly into the ear
of a giggly blonde.

'Rick isn't interested in Selina,' Henry dismissed.

'Oh?' She was regaining control now, wishing she
hadn't made her distress quite so obvious to Rick
Dalmont. He was a man who shouldn't be given any
advantage, and she had just given him one.

'You know he isn't,' her brother sighed.

'Do I?'

'You're too old to play coy games, Shanna,' he said
impatiently. 'The man wants you, and you know it.'

'I also know he isn't going to have me!' Her eyes
flashed deeply green.

'Shanna——'

'Henry, I think we should talk,' she watched his
flushed face warily. 'I don't like the way you've
suddenly become involved with that man.'

'That's business, Shanna——'

'But what business? When did Rick Dalmont
become interested in the world of newspaper publishing?'

'He isn't——'

'Then what business are you involved in with him?'
she frowned.

'We can't talk about it here, Shanna,' he avoided.
'This is a party. And you know Janice doesn't like
business discussed at her parties.'

She sighed. 'Tomorrow, then?'

'Sunday? Mm, come to lunch,' he added. 'Peter and
Susan will like that.'

Her expression softened at the mention of her
nephew and niece. And she had a feeling she was
being manipulated once again, and this time by her
own brother; Henry knew how fond of Peter and
Susan she was.

'We'll talk about Rick Dalmont before lunch.' She

didn't let him even think he had got away with the distraction. 'I'll come over about twelve.'

He grimaced. 'Fine.'

She smiled at his lack of enthusiasm. 'You got into this, Henry,' she drawled at his discomfort. 'Now you can explain it to me.'

'Shanna——'

She touched his cheek mockingly. 'Tomorrow, Henry. And I shall expect a full explanation.'

'But——'

'A full explanation,' she repeated determinedly.

'I'm beginning to wonder who's the eldest in this family,' he muttered before moving away to join his wife, as a couple of the guests were taking their leave.

'A good question,' drawled an amused voice from behind her, an unmistakable voice of honey and gravel. Shanna spun round, wondering just how long Rick Dalmont had been listening to her conversation with her brother.

'You really shouldn't pressurise Henry, honey,' he mocked. 'Now me, you wouldn't have to pressurise at all.'

'I told you——'

'You wouldn't even have to be persuasive,' he cut in softly. 'Let me take you home and I'll tell you all.'

She stiffened at the intimate warmth of his gaze. 'I have my car here.'

He shrugged his broad shoulders. 'Then you drive me home—I came by cab.'

'I'd rather not,' she refused distantly.

Anger flashed in the dark eyes. 'No wonder your husband turned to other women!' he rasped.

Shanna went deathly pale. 'What did you say?'

'When a man is frozen out of his own bed it's inevitable that he'll turn to other women for physical satisfaction,' he scorned.

'Are you saying that's what Perry did?'

'It's public knowledge,' he shrugged again.

'Is it?'

'Was he still sleeping with you before he died?'

'Our sleeping arrangements have nothing to do with—Oh!' she gave a painful gasp as her wrist was grasped and her arm twisted up behind her back, her body brought dangerously close to the hard-muscled flesh of Rick Dalmont. 'Let me go,' she ordered between gritted teeth.

'Smile,' he instructed curtly, his teeth showing white against his dark complexion. 'I said smile, damn it,' he bit out savagely at her lack of response to his order.

She looked about them desperately, amazed that no one could see what this man was doing to her. And then she realised that several people who had come here alone were now in rather close clinches with a man or woman they had met here tonight. Janice would be shocked to know that some of these couples whom she had only just introduced would even be in bed together later tonight.

But not Rick Dalmont and herself. And he was still hurting her, his hold on her arm brutal. 'How can I smile when you're breaking my arm?' she groaned.

He lightened his grip slightly, although the relaxation made her body curve more intimately against him. 'I'm sorry,' but he didn't look very repentant. 'Now answer my question,' he ground out.

'I've forgotten what it was,' she muttered.

'Liar!'

She blinked at the vehemence of his tone. 'I won't discuss my marriage to Perry with you!'

Rick sighed, releasing her completely at the inflexibility of her tone. 'Even in the face of danger you choose to defy me.'

'Danger?' She raised black brows.

'So cool,' he shook his head. 'It isn't natural. Your eyes speak of fire, of all you have to give a man——'

'Not you!'

'Me,' his eyes glittered furiously. 'I'm getting tired of waiting for you, Shanna——'

'What is it, Mr Dalmont?' She refused to rub her aching wrist and arm; she wouldn't show any weakness to this man, ever. 'Did you think that because I've been widowed for the last six months I would fall into your arms like an over-ripe plum? Did you think I would be so sexually frustrated that you would have no trouble at all getting me into bed with you?' Her voice rose angrily.

'Maybe you're sexually cold,' he dismissed.

'Oh, that's usually the next insult!' she scorned. 'Then I'm supposed to sleep with you just to prove that I'm not cold at all. I've been through it all before, Mr Dalmont. I must say, I'm disappointed in you—I expected more sophistication from you.'

His mouth tightened. 'Why do you have to fight me?' he asked quietly, impatiently. 'I've asked you out so many times over the last two weeks that I've lost count.'

'Then give up!'

'I want you, Shanna,' he told her forcefully, pinning her to the spot with the intensity of his gaze. 'And I never give up on something I want as badly as I want you. I've left a trail of broken people behind me who could tell you that.'

She had gone very pale, believing his threat. 'That was business——'

'Business or personal, it doesn't matter,' he shrugged. 'I always win in the end.'

She had heard of his ruthless business dealings, of the people he had ruined in his desire to add to the

Dalmont coffers, but she had never heard of this singlemindedness with a woman before. Although perhaps he had never been turned down before! 'No,' she shook her head. 'Not this time you won't,' she told him with quiet conviction.

'You loved your husband, is that it?'

She couldn't help flinching at the scorn of his tone. 'Yes,' her voice was husky, her head bent.

'You still love him?' he grated.

'Yes.'

'I don't believe it!'

Her head went back proudly, her eyes flashing. 'It's the truth,' she snapped.

'And the parties almost every night, the men who pay you attention—that's mourning him, is it?' Rick derided harshly.

'He wouldn't want me to stay at home.'

'I would!' he bit out fiercely, his eyes jet-black. 'I'd want you to lock yourself away until you died too.'

His intensity took her breath away, and she swallowed hard. 'Maybe that's what I am doing, waiting to die,' she said softly.

'At parties every night?' he scorned.

She looked at him with steady green eyes. 'Maybe I just don't want to be alone when I die.'

Rick Dalmont looked as if she had physically hit him, paling slightly beneath his olive complexion. 'Shanna . . .?'

She sighed, shaking off his hand. 'Selina seems anxious for you to return to her side,' she drawled. 'I'm sure she'll be much more—amenable than I could ever be.'

'I don't want Selina,' he rasped.

'Poor Selina,' she murmured, her cool façade back in place. 'She's very attractive.'

'She doesn't have black hair and green eyes.'

'I'm sure there are thousands of willing women who do.'

'With emphasis on the willing, hmm?' he taunted.

'Exactly.' She gave him a saccharine-sweet smile.

He shook his head. 'It's still you I want, Shanna.'

'I'm sorry.'

'I really believe you are,' he frowned at her quiet sincerity.

'Yes,' she nodded.

'I can't work you out.' Rick shook his head dazedly.

'Don't even try,' she advised. 'Just don't become involved with me——'

'I want to go to bed with you, not become involved!'

Her smile was genuine this time. 'And one precludes the other with you?'

'Yes,' he bit out tautly at her mockery.

'Goodnight, Mr Dalmont. We'll meet again?' she drawled.

'You can bet on it!'

'I'm not usually a betting woman, but I'm sure that if I were I would win that bet.'

'Little tease!' he rasped.

Her humour faded as quickly as it had begun. 'That's one thing I'm not, Mr Dalmont. I've told you bluntly to leave me alone, you've chosen not to take that advice. You would be doing us both a favour, and saving yourself a lot of time, if you gave up on me now.'

'Because you'll never give in to me?'

'No.'

He shrugged. 'I'm not *prepared* to give up on you yet. I'll be seeing you, Shanna.' He ran a fingertip lightly down her cheek, lingering against her mouth, nodding confidently before going over to Henry and Janice to take his leave.

Shanna wasn't altogether surprised at his departure

from the party; he knew there was no point in pursuing her any further tonight, not when she had made her feelings more than plain. And she didn't want to stay here any longer herself now; the verbal encounter with Rick Dalmont had opened up wounds that she knew would never get the chance to heal.

'What did you do to him?' Henry demanded when she joined him. 'I've never known Rick to leave a party at eleven o'clock before!'

She shrugged. 'There has to be a first time for everything.'

'Yes, but——'

'It may have escaped your notice,' she taunted, 'but Selina has gone too.'

'She left with Gary,' her brother dismissed. 'She gave up once Rick returned to you. She decided it's Gary's lucky night instead.'

'Bitchy!' she smiled.

Henry grimaced. 'Selina picks up a different man every time she comes here. I'll have to tell Janice not to invite her again.'

'A snob too!' Shanna mocked.

'Stop changing the subject,' he scowled. 'What did you do to make Rick leave?'

'Nothing.'

'Nothing?' Henry frowned.

'Exactly that,' she nodded. 'And I intend to continue doing nothing. Don't forget to tell Janice I'll be here for lunch tomorrow,' she reminded lightly, intending to show him she had far from forgotten the talk she wanted to have with him.

'She always cooks enough for an army,' he answered vaguely.

Her brother's air of distraction did nothing to reassure Shanna. Henry always knew what he was doing, had been a more than competent successor to their father as head of the family newspaper and magazine empire.

Poor little rich girl, Rick Dalmont had called her. He didn't know anything about her. Until her marriage to Perry four years ago, perhaps that description would have fitted her, but marriage had matured her far beyond the spoilt girl she had been at twenty-one.

She had married Perry against her father's wishes, something that had been hard to do considering her closeness to her single parent, her mother having died years ago. Her father had been completely against her marrying a man who risked his life for a living. But the marriage had been a success, and it had perhaps been Perry's constant brushes with death that had speeded the process of her maturity and cherishing of the deep love they had for each other. Whatever the reason, her father had been assured of her happiness before he died two years ago. At least she had given her beloved father that, and he had been spared the pain she was still suffering, the pain of losing Perry.

No one knew or could understand the loss she felt at Perry's death, not even those closest to her. And no one knew how she feared death for herself . . .

She breakfasted alone the next morning, as she had for the last six months, before tidying the apartment. Not that it needed much of that, one person didn't make much mess, and because she and Perry had spent most of their marriage living out of suitcases she had learnt not to have too many personal possessions, so the apartment was bare of all personal imprint.

It was a new apartment since Perry's death; the one they had used as their home-base when in London had been on the other side of town. But photographs of Perry were prominent in every room, photographs of him racing, of him winning, of the two of them together. Most of them were from before Perry's first accident, the one that had precipitated the end of his career. A serious back injury meant the end of his career as a top racing car driver six months before his death, and she knew it had been a blow Perry had never fully recovered from. Racing had been his life, his career, and for a time he had gone wild.

Damn Rick Dalmont! She knew he was the reason for the memories. What else could she do but remember when he had pointed out so forcibly that all had not been well between Perry and herself at the time of the fatal accident? But he had been right about one thing, the fault in the marriage had been hers, not Perry's. It was true that when a man couldn't find satisfaction in his own bed he turned elsewhere for solace. Perry had done just that.

None of her sleepless night showed as Janice opened the door to her shortly before twelve, her expression coolly composed, looking elegant in a dress the same green of her eyes, its long-sleeved, high-necked style more provocative than a more seductive style could be.

'I'll never know how you do it,' said a harassed-looking Janice, her blonde curls in disarray, a smudge of flour on her nose. 'You always look like a fashion-plate, and I—Well, I look what I am, I suppose, a housewife.'

'A beautiful housewife,' Shanna smiled, kissing her sister-in-law affectionately on the cheek. 'And I look this way because I go out to lunch,' she laughed.

'Hm,' Janice acknowledged wryly. 'Although that doesn't explain how you still look this way when we come to your apartment for dinner too.'

'Caterers,' she taunted dryly.

'You know you're a fantastic cook,' Janice dismissed with a sigh. 'Well, I'd better not keep you from Peter and Susan any longer. They're waiting for you in the lounge.'

The next few minutes were taken up with the ecstatic greetings of her young niece and nephew, although Shanna had time to realise that there was no sign in the spotlessly clean lounge of the smoky party of the night before.

Peter and Susan were five and six respectively, as alike as if they had been twins, both fair-haired and blue-eyed like their mother, although they had their father's height and were both inclined to be serious like Henry too. But they were lovely children, and Shanna greeted them as enthusiastically as they did her.

Henry sat back in his favourite armchair and watched them with an indulgent smile on his lips, puffing away on his favourite pipe, an affectation he believed gave him a look of distinction. It just made him more endearing to Shanna. She and Henry had always been close, despite the difference in their natures, but as the time for lunch neared and Henry still made no effort to bring up the subject of Rick Dalmont she decided to broach the subject herself.

'Henry——'

'Lunch is ready,' Janice came through to announce.

Henry gave a pleased smile as he stood up. 'Thank you, darling.'

'I'll give you thank you!' Shanna muttered as she accompanied her brother through to the dining-room. 'You won't get away so easily after lunch.'

He turned to grin at her. 'But at least then I'll have a full stomach!'

'It won't help you,' she warned.

'Maybe not, but you'll seem less fierce once I've eaten.'

'Fierce, Henry?' she spluttered. 'I've never been fierce in my life!'

He shook his head. 'Sometimes you remind me so much of Dad it's incredible.'

'Dad was a lovely old man, despite his crustiness; I can't see the resemblance at all,' Shanna smiled.

'Oh, it's there. I've seen it in your handling of Rick Dal——'

'——Mont,' she finished triumphantly. 'I'm so glad you haven't forgotten about him, Henry.'

'No,' he mumbled. 'But lunch first, hmm?'

'But no longer,' she warned. 'My patience is wearing a little thin, Henry.'

'I didn't know you had any!'

Shanna grinned at his woebegone expression, and her good humour lasted all through the delicious Sunday lunch Janice had prepared. Peter and Susan helped her with the washing-up afterwards, then she carried through a tray of tea to her brother and Janice, arching her brows at Henry as he seemed settled in front of the television.

'Henry and I will take our tea through to the study,' she announced firmly. 'Won't we, Henry?' She looked at him steadily.

'Will we?' He sighed at her stubborn expression. 'I suppose we will.' He stood up reluctantly.

'I won't keep him long, Janice,' she promised.

'Oh, I think you will,' her sister-in-law said knowingly. 'Good luck, Henry.'

'She sounded as if she thought you might need it,' Shanna questioned as she sat opposite her brother in his study.

'I might,' he nodded.

She frowned. 'Tell me, Henry,' she said quietly, 'what business do you and Rick Dalmont have?'

'You won't like it,' he warned.

'I have a feeling not,' she acknowledged heavily.

He stood up to pace the room. 'You see, the

newspaper hasn't been doing too well lately, and I needed a cash flow for a while.'

'Yes?'

'I've been trying to get this deal together with Rick for months, and when he came over to England two weeks ago it was an ideal opportunity to further the talks. We finalised the deal on Friday, that's partly what the party was about last night.'

'Yes?' Shanna was very wary now. Henry was deliberately avoiding her gaze.

'Well, that's it,' he shrugged.

'No, that isn't it at all, Henry,' she refuted softly. 'You haven't told me anything I didn't already know. What's the deal you've made with Rick Dalmont? Has he come in as your partner or just with a financial loan?'

'Neither.' Henry wetted his lips nervously.

Shanna's unease began to deepen. It wasn't like Henry to be so evasive. 'Then what is the deal?'

'Look, when Dad died he left all the publishing business to me. Maybe he shouldn't have done, but you were happily married to Perry at the time, and Dad did leave you financially secure.'

'I never wanted any of the business, Henry, you know that,' she dismissed. 'You're entitled to make whatever deals you want. I just want to know where I come into it, because I do, don't I?'

'Yes,' her brother sighed heavily. 'It's *Fashion Lady*.'

'What about it?' she gasped.

Henry shrugged. 'As of Friday it belongs to Rick Dalmont. You now work for him.'

CHAPTER TWO

SHANNA's breath left her in a hiss. *Fashion Lady* now belonged to Rick Dalmont! She couldn't believe it. *Fashion Lady* had become her lifeline the last year, had given her something worthwhile to do after Perry's death six months ago. And *Fashion Lady* had continued to thrive under her control, her natural flair for what was fashionable and what would interest the fashion-conscious woman of today increasing the magazine's circulation considerably.

And now it all belonged to Rick Dalmont. 'I'll have to leave,' she said dully.

'Er——'

'Yes?' Her tone was sharp at her brother's hesitation, sensing there was more to come.

Henry looked anxious. 'Part of the deal was that you would stay on for at least a transition period.'

'And how long is that?' she frowned.

'Six months,' he revealed reluctantly.

Shanna rose slowly to her feet. 'No, Henry,' she told him coldly. 'You had no right to sign a deal like that without consulting me. Or were you asked not to?' she realised sharply.

Henry looked sheepish. 'I knew you'd never go for it——'

'*You* knew?' she accused.

'All right, both Rick and I knew.'

'Then you were both right,' she snapped. 'I could never work for him.'

'But I've signed the contracts now!'

'But *I* haven't,' she pointed out stiffly. 'You knew

28

I would never agree to it, Henry,' she shook her head. 'And your signature can't commit me to any-one.'

'You're contracted to *Fashion Lady*, regardless of who owns it.'

'Then I resign,' she snapped.

'Your contract requires three months' notice,' he reminded her.

'I rescind all right to the money owed me,' Shanna told him. 'Just give me my references.'

'I can't do that,' Henry shook his head. 'I'm no longer your employer. And if you leave now Rick would sue you and me for breach of contract.'

'Then let him!' Her eyes flashed in challenge.

'Shanna, I signed my part of the bargain in good faith.' Henry's voice lowered pleadingly. 'One breach of the contract could ruin the whole deal.'

She glared at her brother. 'Then it will have to ruin it!'

'And the *Chronicle* could go under!'

She frowned, searching her brother's face, seeing the lines of worry there, the strain he had been hiding from her. 'That bad?' she said softly.

'That bad,' he nodded grimly.

'Rick Dalmont wouldn't call off the whole deal just because I won't work for him!'

'He will,' Henry said with certainty.

'He—will?'

Her brother nodded. 'He refused to even consider signing the contract until you were included in it.'

'God,' she said shakily.

'It's normal practice for senior staff to stay on after such a negotiation,' Henry pushed his point as he sensed her confusion.

'*Nothing* about Rick Dalmont is normal,' she flashed. 'You know why he's done this, Henry. I won't

go out with him, so he's forcing me to relate to him
from a work point of view.'

'That's rubbish,' he dismissed abruptly. 'I told you,
we've been discussing the deal for months.'

'And when did I enter into it?'

'About—Well, I——' Henry broke off, frowning.

'About two weeks ago, right? Before that I'm sure he
had no interest in the staff of *Fashion Lady*,' she scorned.
'That he didn't give a damn if they stayed or went.'

'That isn't true,' her brother blustered. 'The future
of the staff of *Fashion Lady* has always been high on
my list of priorities.'

'*Your* priorities, Henry,' she pounced triumphantly.
'Rick Dalmont doesn't give a damn about the little
people who get in his way. He told me so himself.'

'No one at *Fashion Lady* is in his way.'

'I will be. His being my boss won't make the
slightest difference to how I feel about him personally.
I don't like him, nothing will change that.'

'You don't have to like him, just work for him.'

'That isn't what he wants, and you know it,' Shanna
sighed. 'Henry, how could you do this to me?' she
groaned. 'You've seen the way he follows me, the way
he never stops looking at me. I'll be handing in my
notice—I have to, Henry,' she insisted as he went to
protest. 'But don't worry, I'll give him his three
months. With any luck he'll leave the acquisition of
Fashion Lady to one of his hirelings.'

But she knew he wouldn't, knew this was just the
opportunity Rick Dalmont had been waiting for. She
wasn't conceited enough to think he had bought
Fashion Lady just to get a hold over her, but she felt
sure he would lose no opportunity in using it as such.
She would have to be very careful of Ricardo Dalmont
in future; he didn't play by any rules she knew, in fact
he didn't play at all!

Everything seemed normal when she went in to work on Monday morning; no high-powered executive was waiting for her to tell her of her new employer. Gloria, her secretary, sat in her normal place behind her desk, handing over the mail and messages that had already come in.

But Shanna knew that she was different, that inside she was a seething mass of emotions. If Rick Dalmont thought he was going to breeze in here and take her by surprise as the new owner of the magazine then he was going to be out of luck; she intended greeting him as coolly as ever. And she didn't intend that he should have the upper hand in anything.

'Gloria,' she buzzed through to her secretary, 'get Mr Dalmont of Dalmont Industries for me. He's at the Excellence, I believe.'

'*Rick* Dalmont?'

'That's the one, Gloria,' she said lightly, releasing the intercom button. Gloria was a good secretary, and had worked for the previous editor too, but even her usually unruffled demeanour had been unnerved by the mention of Rick Dalmont. He would have that effect on most women, and as most of the staff at *Fashion Lady* were women she envisaged more than a little hero-worship once it was known he was the new boss.

'Mr Dalmont, Shanna,' Gloria announced a few minutes later.

She picked up the blue telephone on her desk that matched the blue and white décor of her executive office. The cover of *Fashion Lady* was always in blue and white, and for the most part so was Shanna's office. Blue was a colour she tended to avoid away from work.

'Mr Dalmont?'

'Shanna,' he returned throatily.

'I believe we should meet, Mr Dalmont.' Her tone was briskly businesslike as she imagined his mocking humour at the other end of the telephone.

'You've spoken to Henry?' he drawled.

She could now visualise the look of satisfaction on his smug face. 'I've spoken to him,' she acknowledged. 'Would twelve o'clock in my office be convenient?'

'Are you inviting me out to lunch, Shanna?' he taunted.

Her mouth tightened, the gleam of revenge in her eyes making them glow deeply green. 'I'm inviting you to my office at twelve o'clock,' she told him stiffly.

'I'll be there.' He rang off abruptly.

And so would she. She could sense his feeling of triumph even over the telephone, and she was determined he wouldn't know any more such feelings where she was concerned. He had won this round, and she would see that Henry didn't have to go back on his word as a business man because of her, but Ricardo Dalmont wouldn't win any more rounds over her. She was going to be one step ahead of him from now on. Ignoring him hadn't worked, being polite to him hadn't either, she would have to try and make sure she stayed that one step ahead of him in future.

She had warned Gloria to buzz through to her office when Rick Dalmont arrived, and it was exactly twelve o'clock when the single buzz alerted her. She moved smoothly to her feet, ethereally thin in the black dress, her black hair caught in at her nape, her eyes like twin jewels above her high cheekbones.

Rick Dalmont's eyes widened appreciatively as she went out to greet him, those same dark eyes narrowing at her formality.

'Please come in, Mr Dalmont,' she invited coolly, vaguely irritated by the way Gloria couldn't seem to stop staring at the man. Admittedly he looked very handsome in a fitted iron-grey three-piece suit and snowy white shirt, but he was only a mere man after all. She didn't notice the power that emanated from the force of his body, or the shrewdness in the dark eyes, the determination on the sensuous mouth. She should have noticed all those things about him, but she didn't, was blind to it all. Perhaps if she had noticed . . .

She opened her office door for him to enter, standing back as silence fell over the seven people waiting inside the room, all of them looking at Rick Dalmont with open curiosity. Rick's reaction to this unexpected meeting with *Fashion Lady*'s heads of department was harder to discern, and a hard mask fell over his face as he raised dark brows at her in acknowledgment of the first round going to her.

'We'll discuss this over lunch,' he told her softly, a smile to his lips, only the flare of anger in his dark eyes telling her it would be far from a pleasant conversation.

She moved forward hastily, and silence fell over the room where conversation had begun to buzz as Rick's identity was realised. Her body moved gracefully beneath the black dress, the heels on her sandals adding to her height. 'I'm sure you all know Mr Ricardo Dalmont,' she introduced unnecessarily, knowing that they all realised who he was. 'What you aren't yet aware of is that he is now our new boss.' She turned to him with a challenging smile, the conversation behind her increasing to a roar as the information was absorbed and disbelieved. Like her, her heads of staff had had no idea a takeover was in the offing. Henry had certainly played this close to the ground, and she didn't need two guesses at whose instigation that had been.

Rick met her challenge with an arrogant inclination of his head. 'Mrs Logan has been—premature in her announcement,' he drawled reproachfully. 'I had meant to talk to you all when Mr Blythe was present. But as I was here to take Mrs Logan out to lunch she thought I should have a few words with you before we leave.' It was his turn to give Shanna a challenging look, triumphantly so.

Shanna was so angry that she didn't hear a word he said over the next few minutes, but she could see by the pleased expressions on her colleagues' faces that they liked what he was saying. He might think he had just trapped her into having lunch with him, but he was wrong, no one forced her to do anything she didn't want to do. And she didn't want to have lunch with Rick Dalmont.

'So I can assure you all that I will make as little change in the format of *Fashion Lady* as I can,' he concluded. 'I look forward to working with you, ladies—and gentleman,' he acknowledged the single male head of department in the room with the six ladies. 'A little discrimination in reverse?' he mocked.

Joe Deane gave an appreciative laugh. 'I have no complaints.'

'I don't think I would either.' Rick looked at the women with open appreciation.

'If you've quite finished?' Shanna said icily. 'We still have a magazine to run,' she reminded him curtly.

Rick's eyes narrowed dangerously before he turned to smile at the others. 'I'm sorry I kept you so long,' he told them smoothly. 'I'm sure I'll meet you all later, individually, in the week.'

Shanna could have cringed at some of the open smiles of encouragement on some of the faces of the women she could have sworn were hardbitten career women. Was no woman immune to this man's rakish charm!

'That was not only unethical,' a cold voice of gravel and honey told her softly. 'It was also unprofessional,' Rick bit out tautly; the two of them were completely alone now, and the tension between them was almost unbearable.

'Unprofessional?' she echoed quietly. 'You don't call buying this magazine without even informing the editor unprofessional or unethical?' she demanded angrily.

He shrugged broad shoulders. 'It isn't required of me to tell you anything.'

'Not even when I'm included in the deal?' she snapped.

'As editor of the magazine, of course,' he drawled.

'Of course!'

Again he shrugged. 'It's normal practice——'

'For senior members of staff to stay on after such a negotiation,' she finished dryly. 'You coached Henry very well, Mr Dalmont, he used exactly the same argument.'

'Did it work?' He leant casually back against her desk.

'No!' she told him curtly, holding out an envelope to him. 'I'm giving you three months' notice.'

He took the envelope, putting it away in the breast pocket of his jacket. 'Can you train your replacement in that time?' he enquired coolly.

Shanna bit back her chagrin with effort; he hadn't even tried to talk her out of leaving, damn him. 'I'm sure I can,' she confirmed waspishly.

He nodded. 'I think so too.'

'You don't seem—surprised,' she couldn't prevent the words spilling out of her mouth.

'I'm not,' he shrugged. 'You're an independent lady, you don't like being manoeuvred.'

'You've learnt that much about me at least!' she snapped.

Rick moved closer, his aftershave tangy and pleasant to the senses, as was the good tobacco in the cheroots he smoked, their aroma clinging to his clothing. 'I'd like to learn a lot more about you—if you would let me.'

Her eyes flashed deeply green. 'No!' she took a step away from him. 'I've already told you, I'm not interested. Just leave me alone, Rick.'

'Rick,' he repeated softly. 'I think that's the first time you've ever called me that.' He touched her cheek with gentle fingers. 'It makes a pleasant change after the cold "Mr Dalmont" I've been used to from you.'

She had realised her slip as soon as she said his name. But she was beginning to tire of this man's constant pressure on her; she hadn't slept well the night before, and she felt as jumpy as a kitten about this man as a result of that. 'It won't happen again,' she told him stiffly.

'Won't it?' he derided confidently. 'I have a feeling it will happen a lot in future. You see, I am the new boss around here, and I like my senior *employees* to call me Rick. Let's go to lunch, hmm?' he taunted. 'I have a lot of things to discuss with you.'

'No, I——'

'Concerning the magazine,' he gave her a sideways glance.

Shanna eyed him warily. 'Is that all?'

Dark brows rose mockingly. 'I can't promise not to throw in a few personal remarks of my own, but for the most part—yes, that's all,' he mocked.

'A business lunch?'

'Exactly,' he agreed with satisfaction.

She still didn't trust this man, knew that he was capable of lying to get his own way. But for now she had to fall in with his plans, she owed him a certain amount of loyalty as the new owner of *Fashion Lady*. 'I'll just go and tell Jane I'm leaving,' she nodded coolly.

'Your assistant editor?'

He certainly didn't forget much; she had only briefly introduced him to Jane Meakins, her assistant editor, and yet he had remembered her. She didn't know why that should surprise her; she doubted many things escaped Rick Dalmont's notice. 'I shouldn't be long,' she told him abruptly. 'If you need anything I'm sure my secretary, Gloria, would be pleased to help you,' she added with veiled sarcasm.

'I won't need anything,' he drawled, making himself comfortable in the chair behind her desk.

'Trying it out for size?' she taunted.

He gave her a pitying glance. 'Editor of a women's magazine is not something I had in mind for my future!'

Shanna shot him an impatient look before leaving the room, wondering how one man could induce such violence in her; simply to be with him now made her want to fight or scream at him. And they were both destructive emotions. But also ones that made her feel vibrantly alive, something she hadn't felt for a long time. And she didn't thank Rick Dalmont for arousing such emotions now. Three months of working for him; it could be the longest three months of her life!

He was frowning when she went back into her office several minutes later, standing up ready to leave. 'Do you actually like the décor in this room?' he grimaced.

'It's very—effective.' She shrugged into her jacket with a little help from him, moving away as she realised how close he had suddenly become.

'It's disgusting,' he said bluntly, opening the door for her. 'Your predecessor had abominable taste.'

Her eyes widened as she looked at him. 'How do you know I didn't choose it?'

'You have too much style.' He smiled at her gasp. 'You're a classy lady, Shanna Logan. That's part of your attraction for me. You have style from the tip of your head to your toes.' He handed her into the black London taxi he had miraculously managed to flag down in the busy lunch-hour traffic. 'The Savoy,' he instructed the driver, getting in beside her.

She sat back, very conscious of the length of his thigh pressed against hers as he deliberately sat as close to her as he could, although there was plenty of room on the seat the other side of him. 'You'll have to change your eating habits if you're going to claim this lunch on *Fashion Lady*'s expenses,' she taunted.

His mouth twisted. 'Dalmont Enterprises can pick up the tab for this one,' he smiled. 'And get the decorators into your office first thing tomorrow, will you? It must give you nightmares!'

'Yes,' she admitted reluctantly. 'But Henry always thought it was——'

'Effective,' he echoed her earlier description mockingly.

'Yes,' she confirmed defensively.

Rick Dalmont was obviously known at the Savoy, from the doorman to the maître d', and one of the best tables in the restaurant was made available to them. It obviously paid to have influence and notoriety; the only time she had brought one of the so-called stars here after an interview for the magazine she had had trouble getting a table at all.

'Tell me, Mr Dalmont,' she said once they had ordered their meal. 'If you knew—expected me to hand in my notice, why did you make my being editor part of the deal?' She looked at him with cool green eyes.

He sat back, satisfaction and triumph in every line of his body. 'It gives me three months with you I wouldn't otherwise have had.' He smiled at her puzzled frown. 'Making you – as editor,' he taunted, 'part of the deal, makes you feel obliged to at least work your notice. I'm sure Henry has explained to you the pitfalls of leaving a job without references. Also it could affect the rest of the deal I have with him if you leave now. But I'm sure you know all this, otherwise you would already be walking. Wouldn't you?' he prompted confidently.

'Very clever, Mr Dalmont,' she said tautly.

His mouth quirked. 'Why do I get the impression that was an insult?'

Green eyes clashed with black. 'Because you're a very astute man, Mr Dalmont!'

He laughed softly. 'And you're a fascinating woman, Shanna,' he said without rancour. 'And the name is Rick. I told you, I like all senior members of staff to use it.'

She eyed him sceptically. 'Those poor people you assured you would make no changes to *Fashion Lady*?' she derided hardly.

His mouth tightened. 'You doubt my word?'

Shanna gave him a considering look. 'Not at all. I'm sure that "as little change in the format as you can" will mean exactly that, as little change as *you* can accept until you have the magazine exactly as *you* want it!'

His brows rose in silent appreciation of her deduction, as if he hadn't expected her to be that intelligent.

She sighed. 'I grew up in the world of business, Mr—Rick,' she amended reluctantly. 'My father built up his empire during my childhood, and because my mother died years ago he used to discuss his business with Henry and me.'

'The Stock Exchange for breakfast, hmm?'

'Yes,' she nodded.

'Sounds similar to my own childhood.'

She recoiled from any similarity between herself and this man, regretting telling him even the little she had. 'I doubt it,' she derided. 'We were rich, but not that rich.'

His eyes darkened at the barb, although luckily the arrival of their lunch prevented the biting reply he had looked about to make. 'Let's just enjoy the meal,' he suggested once their food had been served. 'I don't like to argue while I eat.'

'I can't argue with you, I work for you.'

His hand grasped hers as it lay on the table-top. 'At least give me a chance to be pleasant to you. I can assure you I don't usually get as ruthless with women as I have been with you.'

Shanna purposefully disengaged her hand from his. 'As you said, let's eat.'

He gave an impatient sigh, but as he picked up his cutlery she knew they were to at least eat in peace.

'What do you think of Jane for my replacement?' she asked as they drank their coffee, having decided it was time for the 'business' discussion he had asked for.

Rick frowned, giving the idea some thought. 'No,' finally came his blunt answer.

She held back her sharp retort with effort. When she had taken over *Fashion Lady* a year ago Henry had more or less given her complete control, to do what she felt best for the magazine, to make what decisions she felt were necessary, and without being conceited she knew that the majority of them had been the right decisions. For her to have consulted Rick Dalmont at all just now had been hard enough, to have him turn down her suggestion so emphatically was a damned insult.

'Why not?' she snapped in challenge.

He shrugged. 'I want someone with a new approach, not a staff member who still has her loyalties to you and the new projects you started.'

'Then you agree I've given *Fashion Lady* some input?' Her sarcasm was barely contained.

Rick raised dark brows at her vehemence. 'It's good to see that something can fire your interest.'

'Plenty of things do that, Mr Dalmont!'

'But not me?'

'No, not you! Now about Jane——'

'I said no,' he rasped.

'And that's the last that will be said on the subject?' she scorned.

'Yes!'

She drew in a deep controlling breath. 'Very well,' her tone was once again cold and remote, 'I'll see about advertising for a replacement.'

'It was your decision to leave, Shanna,' he reminded softly.

'And I don't regret it for a moment!' She stood up. 'If you'll excuse me, my lunch-hour was over long ago.'

Rick stood up too, putting some money down on the table to cover the bill. 'I didn't think you had noticed,' he taunted, his hand firm on her elbow as they left the restaurant together.

'I noticed,' she derided. 'But it's your time . . .'

'In that case,' his mouth tightened, 'I'd like you to spend the afternoon with me at my hotel, discussing business, of course.'

'Of course,' she said dryly. 'I have too much to do at the office, Mr Dalmont,' she refused.

'Some other time, eh?' he mocked.

'I doubt it.'

'So do I,' he grinned, suddenly looking younger. 'I

wish you would reconsider your decision to leave, Shanna. With a few changes, and your dedication,' he taunted, '*Fashion Lady* could become the top women's magazine in the country.'

'I doubt I would like your changes, Mr Dalmont.'

'Even if they are for the good of *Fashion Lady*?' His eyes were narrowed.

'In your opinion!' she scorned. 'Since when did you become an expert on publishing, Mr Dalmont?'

'Since I bought *Fashion Lady* and made it my business to be!' he snapped angrily, stopping a passing taxi to open the door for her to get inside, leaning on the open window after closing the door behind her. 'I'll be seeing you, Shanna,' he told her grimly before nodding to the driver to take her back to her office.

Shanna stared straight ahead as the taxi moved off into the heavy London traffic, knowing Rick Dalmont's last words had been in the form of a threat. She would indeed be 'seeing' him—he would make sure of that.

It wasn't until she got back to her office that she realised that, except for her asking about Jane, they hadn't discussed business at all during lunch. Rick Dalmont was more than distrustful, he was dangerous!

'What a shock!' Jane came into her office on her return. 'I had no idea *Fashion Lady* was for sale.'

Shanna grimaced. 'Neither did I until yesterday.'

Jane's eyes widened. She was a pretty woman in her early twenties, the same as Shanna, her blonde hair kept short and easily styled, her make-up light and attractive, her clothes always fashionably smart. 'Henry didn't tell you?' She sounded surprised.

'Not until it was too late.'

'Mm—well, Mr Dalmont does have the financial backing *Fashion Lady* needs.'

She frowned. 'You don't mind that he's the new boss?'

Jane shrugged. 'I know it must be difficult for you, with Henry being your brother, but a boss is a boss as far as I'm concerned. The way things are for unemployment in this country at the moment we're all lucky to have jobs at all.'

Jane's down-to-earth attitude was something she needed at the moment. They *were* all lucky to have a job, and jobs as editors didn't come along every day; she doubted she would be lucky enough to find another one, even *with* references.

It was something that bothered her as she prepared to go out later that evening. Financially she didn't need to work, both Perry and her father had left her very well off, but mentally and emotionally...? Heavens, she couldn't spend her days sitting around the apartment just counting the minutes away! That would only lead to thoughts of Perry, of the last traumatic months of their marriage.

Damn, she was thinking about it already! She had taken great care to fill all of her time, with work in the day, sometimes until she felt like collapsing, and with a round of parties in the evenings. She rarely gave herself time to think, let alone dwell on the past.

And tonight would be no exception! So she would be out of a job in three months; she would find something else, she would make sure she did.

She looked her usual cool and composed self later that evening when she arrived at Steven and Alice Grant's for dinner. The middle-aged couple were old friends of her father's, and her own friendship with them had continued even after his death. This evening was a celebration of their twenty-fifth wedding anniversary, and she knew Alice was pleased with the jade figurine Shanna had given her to add to her already extensive collection.

She already knew most of the other guests at the Grant house, and made a beeline for her brother as she spotted him across the room, a smiling Janice at his side.

'Going somewhere?' drawled the familiar gravel and honey voice that she was beginning to feel was haunting her.

She schooled her features to remain calm, turning slowly to face Rick Dalmont. Goodness, he was dressed to kill tonight! The black velvet jacket fitted smoothly across his powerful shoulders, the white of his shirt making his skin appear swarthier than ever, his black trousers moulded to the lean length of his long legs. His dark eyes were filled with amusement as he met and held her gaze, his black hair brushed back from its side-parting to rest low over his ears and collar. He held a drink in his hand, evidence that he had been here for some time.

'Good evening, Mr Dalmont,' she greeted softly.

He moved closer to her. 'Hello, Shanna.'

'We do seem to—keep meeting.'

'No, we don't *seem* to do anything,' he drawled. 'But then I'm sure you already knew that.'

'Steven and Alice are friends of yours?' She ignored the intimacy of his tone.

He shook his head. 'I've never met them before this evening.'

She gasped. 'You gatecrashed their party?'

His mouth quirked. 'I came with Henry and Janice.'

Shanna's mouth tightened as she shot a resentful glare at her unsuspecting brother. 'I should have known! Well, if you'll excuse me——'

'No,' his hand on her arm stopped her leaving. 'I'm still trying to be pleasant, as I tried at lunchtime,' he smiled tightly. 'But you angered me then, and you're angering me now,' he added tautly. 'What do you think I can possibly do to you here, Shanna?' He looked pointedly about the crowded room.

She blushed at the rebuke of his words, and knew she was behaving ridiculously. There were at least forty people in the room; not even Rick Dalmont would try anything here.

'Exactly,' he correctly read her thoughts. 'Although most women don't show such aversion to the thought of my wanting to make love to them.'

'I'm not most women,' she snapped.

'I agree, you aren't.' He took her hand and placed it in the crook of his arm, holding it there with his other hand. 'Which probably accounts for the way I ache for you,' he lowered his voice seductively. 'Put my plain speaking down to my Spanish ancestry,' he chuckled at her tight-lipped outrage. 'I want you very badly, Shanna.'

'You told me that the other evening,' she dismissed abruptly. 'And what you're talking about is sex, Mr Dalmont, not making love.'

'The way I would worship your body it would be making love,' he murmured against her earlobe.

'I——'

'Ah, Shanna, you found Rick,' Alice Grant, an attractive woman in her late forties, beamed at them both. 'With the rush of the Sinclairs arriving at the same time as you I completely forgot to tell you Mr Dalmont had already arrived with Henry,' she told Shanna hurriedly. 'And how silly of you to think we wouldn't have room for your—for Rick,' she corrected awkwardly. 'We've all been so worried about Shanna, Mr Dalmont,' she confided to the silently watchful man at Shanna's side. 'We all miss Perry enormously, but Shanna really is too young and lovely a woman to deny her company to some lucky man.'

Much as she liked Alice Grant, who was the nearest

thing she had to an aunt, Shanna could cheerfully have strangled her at that moment. And this 'lucky man' was going to be told a few home truths as soon as they were alone! How dared he have implied to Alice that he was her partner for this evening!

'I do consider myself very lucky, Mrs Grant,' Rick drawled confidently. 'And I've also been very worried about Shanna. But she has me now, don't you, sweetheart?' He looked down at her in mocking challenge.

Anger lit up her eyes. 'I——'

'Ah, the Daniels have arrived,' Alice sighed her relief. 'Steven's boss,' she confided softly. 'I'll talk to you both later,' and she hurried to be at her husband's side as he greeted the other couple.

Shanna wrenched away from Rick Dalmont, breathing deeply in her agitation. 'What did you tell Alice when you arrived?' she demanded to know.

He met her gaze with bland innocence. 'That you were working late and would meet me here as soon as you could get away.'

'You—I—And Henry went along with that?' she gasped indignantly.

'Why not?' he shrugged. 'I told him the same thing when I spoke to him on the telephone and he told me you were all going to a dinner party this evening.'

'You arrogant—My God, I can't believe this!' she shook her head. 'You have the cheek of the devil!'

He nodded. 'Some people have even claimed we're related,' he said with amusement. 'But I doubt Alice would understand if you tried to explain the true facts to her. She's a romantic lady, and she thinks that by seeing me you're finally getting your life back together after your husband's death. Don't ruin her evening, will you?' he mocked.

'What about mine?' she bit out.

'Yours is already ruined,' he shrugged dismissively. 'Look, I'll be on my best behaviour, okay?'

'That isn't good enough! I don't——'

'Behave yourself!' Rick rasped as Henry and Janice walked over to join them. 'Save your insults for when we're alone and stop behaving like a child! Just think of this as an exercise in employer/employee relations.'

'I don't want any sort of "relations" with you,' she snapped.

He gave her a mocking smile before turning to charm her brother and Janice. The last thing she needed was an example of his lethal charm at work, and she was too angry to notice the curious looks her brother kept shooting her. And she didn't *want* to feel angry either, didn't want to feel anything for this man, not even dislike.

'By the way, Henry,' Rick gave Shanna a sideways glance, 'Shanna has already introduced me to some of the staff at *Fashion Lady*.'

Henry frowned his puzzlement. 'She has?'

'Mm,' Rick nodded. 'Only casually, of course, on our way out to lunch.'

Henry looked even more puzzled. And well he might after her vehement avowal of dislike of Rick Dalmont over the weekend. To all intents and purposes she had already lunched with him today, and now she was spending the evening with him too!

Rick's arm moved about her waist, pulling her close against his side. 'And how could I resist your sister when she asked me out so persuasively?' he added throatily.

'*Shanna* invited *you* out to lunch?' Henry was astounded—and unable to hide it.

Before Shanna could defend any such misconception dinner was announced, and to her chagrin Alice had put Rick Dalmont next to her at the table. His smile of triumph was enough to make her ignore him throughout the meal, although this only seemed to amuse him. Trying to reject this man was like hitting her head against a brick wall, and she just didn't know what to do next. How pleased he would be if he even knew he was succeeding that far!

'I like your friends,' he told her as they circulated after the meal, his hand on her arm refusing to be shaken off as she would have gone alone to speak to Henry and Janice.

'They like you too,' she muttered, knowing he had been at his most pleasant as they spoke to the people she knew at this dinner party, his hold on her enough claim of possession for him at the moment. In this lazily charming mood it would be difficult for anyone to dislike him, but she knew the other side of him too well to be fooled for a moment; when thwarted this man was lethal. 'I think I'd like to leave now,' she said tightly.

'What a good idea,' he nodded. 'Let's go and make our excuses.'

'You don't have to leave with me,' she faced him.

He quirked one dark brow. 'Now wouldn't it look a little odd if you left and I stayed?'

'That didn't seem to bother you earlier when you arrived without me!'

'Ah, but I had a good excuse for that.' He looked at her mockingly.

'All right,' she agreed tightly. 'We'll leave together.'

'Could I have a word with Henry before we go?'

'Why not?' Her voice was taut, her nerves at breaking point. 'You seem to do everything else you want to!'

Rick laughed softly. 'I'm glad you realise it.'

'*Almost* everything,' she amended hardly.

His chuckle deepened. 'Let's go and see Henry,' he prompted lightly.

Her brother was looking very pleased with himself when they joined his group, and Shanna didn't need two guesses as to the reason for that; he believed she had decided to accept Rick Dalmont after all. She could have told him she intended leaving Rick Dalmont as soon as they were out of Steven and Alice's door, and she didn't intend being caught in this position again. So much for keeping one step ahead!—she had taken half a dozen backwards this evening.

CHAPTER THREE

'I JUST wanted to remind you that you're taking me round *Fashion Lady* tomorrow at ten,' Rick told Henry a few minutes later; the four of them were now alone.

This was news to Shanna, and she decided to listen to the rest of their conversation in case there was something else she didn't know either!

Henry frowned. 'But I thought Shanna had already——'

'Your sister just sprang a little surprise introduction for me,' Rick drawled, enjoying the cold look she gave him. The reason he had mentioned *Fashion Lady* was now becoming apparent; he hoped to embarrass her in front of Henry. 'I wasn't quite prepared for it,' he continued lazily. 'But I think I handled it okay.'

He had more than handled it okay, and he knew it! He had been so charming, so easygoing and assured, that there had been none of the uncertainty and resentment that usually initially went along with a take-over like this. Most of the staff she had spoken to had reacted with the same untroubled acceptance that Jane had.

But Rick's lazily drawled words now had aroused Henry's suspicions, and she could see him mentally adding up the situation—and arriving at the right answer!

'We'll be round at ten in the morning, Shanna,' Henry told her curtly, 'when I'll give Rick the official introduction to the staff that he deserves.'

It took a lot to anger her usually even-tempered

brother, but she could see that her method of dealing with Rick Dalmont over his acquisition of *Fashion Lady* had far from met with Henry's approval. It had backfired on her anyway. Rick's arrogant assurance was such that nothing unsettled him.

'We'll be ready,' she told her brother softly, a plea for understanding in her eyes. He gave her an impatient look, shaking his head in silent reproach. She turned away, her mouth tight.

'I think I've already had the introduction to the staff of *Fashion Lady* that Shanna thinks I deserve,' Rick drawled tauntingly, enjoying her discomfort.

She turned blazing green eyes on him. She didn't mind that he mocked her, and if they were alone she would probably have given back as good as he was giving. But as he was five years her senior, and the only close family she had left, she valued Henry's liking and respect for her as a businesswoman as well as his sister. He had taken a chance on her with *Fashion Lady*, a chance that had, luckily, paid off. Her behaviour this morning might have been petty and spiteful, but she didn't appreciate Rick telling Henry about it; the argument between the two of them was strictly private!

'I shall be honoured to show you round the magazine tomorrow, Rick,' she told him coolly. 'There really isn't any need to bother Henry.'

'I'll be there,' her brother told her grimly. 'It's only protocol that the previous owner should introduce the new one.' He gave her another disapproving glare.

'Shanna wants to leave,' Rick spoke smoothly. 'So we'll say goodbye now.'

She seethed inside all the time they were making their farewells to Steven and Alice, wrenching out of his grasp as soon as they were outside, the cool evening air making her huddle down in her velvet jacket. 'That was the most despicable, rotten——'

'I know, I know,' Rick interrupted her tirade impatiently. 'But what you did this morning wasn't according to the rules of the game.' He held her in front of him, his eyes very dark in the light flowing from the house behind them. 'I like to keep business and pleasure completely separate, but this morning you crossed over that line.'

'Because you'd already done so!' She was taut with tension. 'You did so the moment you included me in your contract with Henry.'

'I've been making the arrangements to buy *Fashion Lady* for months.'

'And two weeks ago you suddenly decided I should be included in it!'

His mouth tightened. 'Henry has a big mouth,' he ground out.

'He's my brother!'

'He's also a businessman!'

Her mouth twisted with scorn. 'You may be able to separate your priorities into such defined categories, Mr Dalmont,' she ignored the warning narrowing of his eyes at her formality, 'but I can't—and neither, thank God, can Henry.'

There seemed to be a mental battle going on behind the dark eyes, until finally Rick sighed. 'I warned you there would be retribution for this morning, so now we're even,' he shrugged dismissively.

'No, we are not even,' she bit out in a controlled voice. 'I don't want to be even with you, I don't want to be anything with you. What I did this morning you deserved, what you've done, making me work for you, invading my life like you did tonight, I've done nothing to deserve.'

'You're too damned beautiful,' he rasped.

Her eyes widened. 'I have to be punished for *that*?'

'Working for me won't be a punishment!' His expression softened from anger. 'It could be very— rewarding, if you would let it be.'

Shanna drew in an angry breath. 'I believe this is sexual harassment, and I have a right to——'

'Sexual harassment!' he exploded, his eyes black, his mouth grim. 'I've never had to harass a woman into bed with me!'

'Then you're giving a very good impression of it!'

Black eyes warred with green for several long tension-filled minutes, until Rick finally sighed his exasperation with her. 'I don't intend arguing out here with you,' he reasoned. 'For one thing it's too damned public, and for another it's too cold. The dampness of the weather here gets into my bones,' he grimaced. 'We can talk in the car. Which one is yours?' There were almost two dozen cars parked down the driveway.

'Mine?' she echoed sharply. 'But you——'

'I told you, I came with Henry and Janice, and I meant that literally. I took a cab to their place and drove here with them.'

'But——'

'Which is your car, Shanna?' he rasped impatiently. 'Before we both freeze to death!'

'The brown Mercedes sports car. But——'

He took the car keys out of her hand, striding purposefully over to her car to unlock the door, and sliding in behind the wheel. Shanna stood indignantly beside the car, glaring down at him as he switched on the engine.

'Well, get in,' Rick indicated the passenger door he had opened for her.

'You're in my seat,' she ground out.

He relaxed back against the leather. 'I never allow a

woman to drive me,' he drawled. 'Not since my mother told me she always thinks out the day's menus as she drives.'

'Well, I don't. And I——'

'No, you probably organise the layout for the readers' letters while you drive,' he taunted. 'It's just a question of differing values.'

Shanna knew she was occasionally guilty of letting her mind wander as she drove, but she was sure it wasn't a practice limited to women as Rick seemed to imply it was! 'And you probably think of the next woman you're going to bed with!' she snapped waspishly, getting into the car beside him, only just managing to fasten her safety belt before he put the Mercedes in gear and drove off.

He turned to give her a confident smile. 'You're never far from my mind, Shanna,' he mocked.

She turned away, her mouth tight, deciding to end the intimacy of *that* conversation. 'I don't remember ever offering to drive you home.'

'But you aren't—I'm driving you.'

And very capably too. Perry had been a good driver, but his skill on the race-track, his enjoyment of speed, had occasionally spilt over during his normal driving, and that didn't make for an enjoyable drive. Rick Dalmont drove with ease and the minimum of effort, instilling confidence in his passengers. But she shouldn't have been the passenger, damn him!

'Would you mind?' A gold cigarette case appeared in her vision, and she looked up to see Rick was holding it out to her. 'Could you get me a cheroot out—please?' he added in a cajoling voice as he saw the hardening of her mouth.

She did so with little grace, watching as he put the dark cheroot between his teeth.

'Could you light it for me too?' He handed her a

lighter that matched the cigarette case he was now sliding back into the breast pocket of his jacket.

She sat forward to click the lighter to a flame beneath the cheroot, her mouth unsmiling as she gave it back to him to put away.

'Of course I could have done it myself,' he told her conversationally a few seconds later, 'but I'm desperate enough to want you to perform any little intimate task for me.' He glanced at her sideways. 'And there's something very intimate about what you just did.'

'Really?' she drawled uninterestedly, burning inside with indignation.

'Yes,' he mocked softly. 'Admit it, Shanna, you liked me a little better tonight.'

'I'll admit nothing of the sort! You're a manoeuvring, arrogant bast——'

'Do you usually call your boss a bastard?' he rasped.

'I've only ever had one other boss, and I know for a fact that Henry is legitimate.'

'He's also given you too much freedom,' Rick snapped. 'I would hazard a guess that most of the men in your life have allowed you too much of your own way. First your father and brother, then your husband. And now there's me.'

'You certainly couldn't be accused of being indulgent!' There were two bright spots of angry colour in her cheeks.

'I can be—at the right time, in the right place,' Rick taunted. 'Now we're in the right place, I just have to persuade you it's the right time.'

He had halted the car outside one of London's quietly exclusive hotels and was already getting out from behind the wheel, coming round to open her door for her.

Shanna stood next to him on the pavement. 'If you'll just give me my car keys . . .'

'I thought we could have a drink before you leave.'

'No, thank you.' She held out her hand for the keys.

Rick made a point of putting them in his trouser pocket. 'Just one drink?'

'No!' She met the challenge in his dark eyes, seeing he wasn't about to give in. 'I'll get a taxi home,' she decided tautly.

'Good idea.' He took the steps two at a time to the glass doors that led into the hotel, pausing to turn and look at her. 'I'll bring your car to the *Fashion Lady* offices in the morning when I meet Henry. Of course he could be curious as to how I come to have your car, but I'm sure I can come up with some viable explanation for that.' He was whistling tunelessly beneath his breath as he allowed the doorman to open the door for him, cheerfully nodding his thanks as he went inside.

Shanna watched him go with a feeling of a trap closing about her. Rick Dalmont was a manipulating swine, but at the moment he held all the top cards.

Her heels clicked angrily as she ran up the stairs to find the door already being held open for her; the man's expression was deadpan, telling her that he had overheard most if not all of the conversation between Rick and herself. Her head went back defensively as she saw Rick leaning against the lift door to keep it open for her.

'Relax, Shanna,' he drawled as she reached his side. 'This is a hotel, not an apartment. We can even have that drink in the lounge if you like.' He stepped into the lift, pressing the hold button as she made no effort to join him. 'The lounge and bar are upstairs,' he mocked.

She stepped in beside him silently, her face averted as she felt his taunting gaze on her.

'One drink and then you can have your keys back,'

he told her softly as the lift doors opened and he stepped out.

Shanna followed him down the carpeted corridor. The luxury of the hotel meant nothing to her; she and Perry had stayed in plenty of them during their tours of the race circuit.

Rick unlocked the door to a room, gently pushing her inside before switching on the lights. It was obviously a hotel suite and not a public lounge at all.

She turned to him accusingly. 'You said——'

'I said a lounge and a bar,' he held up his hands defensively. 'This is the lounge of my suite, and over there is the bar,' he pointed to the extensive bar in the corner of the room.

'You lied by omission,' she said tautly.

'I didn't lie at all,' he told her slowly. 'I've been honest with you from the beginning—about everything. Now, what would you like to drink?'

'Nothing. I'd like my car keys so that I can leave.' She stood in the middle of the room, the dark green velvet jacket she wore darkening her hair to the same black as her dress, her eyes a deep glowing green.

'No drink?' Rick took a step towards her.

She stood her ground, proudly erect. 'Just the keys.'

'You can have them back——' he stood only inches away from her now, his warmth reaching out to her, the tangy smell of his aftershave and the faint aroma of the cheroots he smoked discernible to her—'if you'll give me one kiss first,' he prompted softly.

'No,' she scorned.

'Then no keys,' he shrugged.

'Mr Dalmont——'

'Shanna,' he mocked.

'This is blackmail,' she snapped.

'You see what you've made me resort to,' he groaned.

'I think I'd rather get a taxi and let Henry make his own assumption about why you have my car,' she turned away.

'No!' Rick pulled her round roughly. 'No, Shanna, I can't let you go . . .' His head bent down and his mouth captured hers.

She knew that fighting him would do no good as soon as she felt the steel of his body in front of her and the strength of his arms about her. The only alternative was to limply accept the assault on her mouth by his, to offer no resistance as he probed her lips to search her mouth, drinking deeply of the warm recesses.

'Kiss me back, damn you,' he raised his head enough to rasp, a wild light of recklessness in his black eyes. 'I've got you this far, you aren't going to leave now!' His mouth claimed hers once again, ravaging her softness, desperately trying to evoke a response from her.

And she couldn't give him one, wouldn't give him one. This man was taking, he wasn't giving, and she wouldn't give to him either.

'Damn you!' he finally thrust her away from him, turning his back on her. 'Go if you want to!'

'I want to.' Shanna straightened the smoothness of her silky hair, moistening her lips, already feeling their tenderness from his onslaught. 'My keys,' she reminded him.

He thrust his hand into his pocket, throwing the keys at her. 'Drive carefully,' he muttered as she walked towards the door.

His concern stopped her in her tracks, and she looked at him dazedly. 'Rick . . .?'

He turned, taking a deep breath, running a hand through his hair and ruffling its darkness. 'I'm trying to be a good loser,' he told her ruefully. 'It just isn't a role I'm used to,' he said without conceit.

His lack of apology was enough to break the tension between them, and her mouth quirked into a smile of amusement. 'Humility certainly doesn't become you!'

'No,' he sighed. 'Neither does sexual disappointment. I need a cold shower.'

Shanna was smiling openly now. 'Does that really work?'

Rick grimaced. 'I'll know that later.'

'Having no previous experience, hmm?'

'None,' he drawled.

'No one could ever accuse you of being modest,' she taunted.

Rick shrugged. 'No one has ever wanted to.'

'You're incredible!' she gasped.

'Incredible as in amazing, or incredible as in arrogant? No, don't answer that, I can guess.' He shook his head. 'You do nothing for my ego, Shanna.'

'It doesn't sound as if your ego needs anything doing for it. There are millions of women out there,' she indicated the rest of the world. 'Go after one of them, Rick. Please!'

'I can't.'

'You can! There must be——'

'I can't, Shanna,' he repeated softly. 'My reputation is going to suffer, you know,' he added lightly as he sensed her tension rising once again. 'My ladies don't usually leave ten minutes after they arrive.'

'Maybe they weren't really ladies,' she said curtly.

'Maybe not,' he conceded. 'Come on, I'll walk down to the car with you.' He grasped her elbow, taking her to the door.

She shook her head. 'That isn't necessary.'

'My mama would never forgive me for not seeing a lady to her car,' he derided.

She shrugged acceptance, knowing that to argue with him would do no good; this man was a law unto himself. 'I didn't realise your mother was still alive,' she told him as they went down in the lift.

'Both my parents are,' he nodded. 'Dad retired fifteen years ago to spend more time with Mama. She has a heart complaint,' he frowned. 'My father is almost twenty years older than she; she was only eighteen when they got married, and yet Mama is probably going to die first. I don't think my father ever expected that.'

'I'm sorry.'

'Yes, so am I,' his voice had hardened, too intent on his own thoughts to notice how much she had paled. 'They've been in love almost forty years, I don't know what Dad will do when he's on his own.' His expression became closed as they walked across the foyer and out to her car. 'I didn't mean to bore you with my family history,' he said as he opened her door for her.

'You didn't bore me,' she said slowly.

'No?' he grimaced at her air of preoccupation. 'You're giving a good impression of it.'

'No, I——' She broke off, biting her lip. 'I'd better go,' she told him lightly. 'My new boss is coming to the office tomorrow; I have to be fresh and alert for him.'

Rick returned her smile. 'I'd rather you were soft and kittenish, maybe a little sleepy, after a night in my bed.'

He made the statement in the form of a question, and for her answer Shanna switched on the ignition. 'I'll see you in the morning, Mr Dalmont.'

'Ten o'clock—Mrs Logan,' he taunted, stepping away from the car.

Rick would have been right in his assessment of her mind not being on her driving as she went home—it was far removed from that! After the way Rick had kissed her, forced his passion on her, she had been ready to walk out of his hotel room hating him more than ever, but listening to him talking about his parents, his obvious concern for his mother, somehow made him seem less the arrogant Rick Dalmont and more Ricardo, the son of Teresa. And that could be dangerous for her, could break down all the defences she had built up this last year, the defences she needed to get her through the rest of her life.

Henry's telephone call to her office at five past nine the next morning wasn't exactly unexpected. 'What you did yesterday was childish, Shanna,' he told her crossly. 'It was also unprofessional.'

'So Rick told me,' she said dryly.

'Yes—well, he was right!' her brother regained some of his composure. 'But at least he's willing to forget about it.'

'How do you know that?' she asked in a surprised voice.

'Well, the two of you had lunch together, and you were together last night too.'

'Yes, but—Yes,' she sighed. 'Although you shouldn't read too much into that, Henry.'

'Everyone else at the party was. Rick isn't known for his consistency with women, and yet he didn't leave your side all night.'

'One evening doesn't constitute a change in his character,' she derided.

'You're hardly giving the man a chance, Shanna.'

She gave an impatient sigh. 'You could be his P.R. man, Henry,' she taunted bitterly. 'But I have no intention of giving him or any other man "a chance". Perry's only been dead six months, I thought you had more loyalty to him than that.'

'I have,' he sighed. 'I liked Perry, you know that, we

all did. It's just—things were far from smooth between you before he died. You're still young, Shanna, you deserve to still have a life of your own.'

'I have a life. I work. I go out——'

'Always alone,' he pointed out.

'I prefer to be alone.'

'That's my whole point——'

'And you've completely missed mine,' she snapped. 'I lost my husband only six months ago. I loved Perry very much, Henry.'

'I know,' he acknowledged quietly. 'But the way he treated you before he died . . .!'

'He loved me,' she insisted.

'I know that too. But there are different ways of loving. Perry loved you while the marriage and his career were going well. But after the first accident, when he couldn't race any more, he treated you abominably.'

'He was lost without his racing——'

'He had you!'

'And it wasn't enough!' she said heatedly. 'It wouldn't be for a lot of men. I understood what he went through, you didn't, so don't presume to judge him on what you do know. Perry loved me, he never stopped loving me. And I loved him. I don't want to talk about it any more,' she added abruptly. 'And I don't want to discuss Rick Dalmont any more either. He wants a quick affair and I don't, that's the end of it.'

'Shanna——'

'I mean it, Henry,' she told him in a softly controlled voice. 'One more criticism against Perry and you're going to find this office empty when you arrive with Rick at ten o'clock,' she warned.

'I'm not criticising him,' her brother defended. 'I'm trying to understand.'

And he never would, no one would, because no one knew the whole truth about Perry's first accident, or their six months of marriage after that. And no one ever would!

'I'll see you and Rick at ten o'clock, Henry,' she said curtly.

'Shanna——'

'Ten o'clock.' She rang off abruptly, lacing her fingers together to stop her hands from shaking.

For six months she had lived without curiosity or probing from her older brother, knowing that he respected the privacy of the problems in her marriage before Perry died. In just two weeks Rick Dalmont had shaken her whole life upside down, was forcing her out from behind the wall she had built over her emotions. Until she met him two weeks ago she hadn't felt love and she hadn't felt hate, she had lived her life day after day, often wishing that Perry hadn't died alone in that second accident, that she didn't have to spend the rest of her life without him.

But Rick Dalmont wasn't going to let her stay behind that wall; he had even involved Henry on his side of the argument. Some of the foundations might be a bit shaky, but she would soon build the wall back up again—she had to!

No one could have faulted her manner or appearance as she welcomed her brother and Rick into her office at exactly ten o'clock. Her manner was coolly polite, her dress a deep shade of burgundy, giving an ebony sheen to her hair.

But Rick wasn't at all deterred by her coolness, grinning at her unabashedly as he mocked, 'And are you feeling fresh and alert this morning, Shanna?'

She looked at him with unflinching green eyes, subconsciously wondering how he managed to look so much more impressive in his navy suit than Henry did in his. The two men were of a similar build, both tall and powerfully built, but there the similarity ended; Rick Dalmont possessed an elegance and style Henry could never hope to achieve.

'Yes, thank you, Mr Dalmont,' she replied distantly.

One dark brow quirked mockingly. 'I think I would still prefer you soft and kittenish,' he taunted.

'And I still prefer my own bed!'

'You should have said so,' he drawled. 'I had no preference as to the bed we used.'

The embarrassed colour in her brother's cheeks reached the tip of his ears, and Shanna's coolness had turned to anger. How dared he talk to her this way in front of Henry! One look into the black eyes told her that he would dare more than that if he had to.

She stood up, unconsciously graceful in her movements. 'If you're ready for the tour,' she said pointedly.

'Any time you are,' he mocked.

'Now,' she said abruptly, moving to the door. But Rick was there before her, holding it open for her, a teasing quirk to his mouth. She chose to ignore it, sweeping past him with cool disdain.

She had to admire him during the next hour, the way that he obviously had done his homework on publishing; all the questions he asked, of Henry and herself, and also of the people in the different departments who now worked for him, were very relevant and knowledgeable. Rick Dalmont was obviously a man who didn't ask someone to do something if he wasn't well aware beforehand that it could be done, even if it might be difficult. He was like a sponge, absorbing and filing away each piece of information he received for future reference.

'It looks good, Henry,' he told her brother when they returned to Shanna's office for coffee. Gloria was so agog with curiosity about their new boss when she brought in the tray, she almost walked into the door on her way out, although Rick didn't seem to notice her.

Henry nodded. 'Your lawyers did a pretty thorough job of investigating before you bought *Fashion Lady*.'

'They always do,' the other man nodded, his gaze warm as Shanna handed him his cup of coffee. 'Thanks, sweetheart.'

She stiffened at the endearment, although Henry seemed not to notice anything unusual about a boss calling an employee 'sweetheart'. It made her realise that her brother still harboured some hope that she would come to like the other man.

'Surely *Fashion Lady* is rather small for the head of Dalmont Industries to interest himself in personally?' she prompted abruptly.

Cool black eyes were turned on her. 'When *Fashion Lady* is being run as I want it to be perhaps I'll move on, but until that time it remains my prime project.'

And you along with it! his eyes seemed to say. Shanna turned away, making a point of serving her brother his coffee.

'Will you be making many changes?' Henry asked interestedly.

'Some.' The other man didn't elaborate.

'Shanna has done a good job this last year.'

'I agree,' Rick nodded.

'But?' she prompted softly.

'I don't believe I said "but".' His black eyes taunted her.

'Then you should have,' she challenged.

He gave an inclination of his head, his smile mocking her. 'Perhaps I should,' he agreed, again not elaborating any further.

'Well?' she prompted after a lengthy silence.

'Well,' he nodded, obviously enjoying himself—at her expense.

Her mouth tightened. 'Just tell me if anyone is going to lose their job in this shake-up.'

Rick met her gaze steadily. 'I don't have to tell you anything, Shanna. You'll know any management decisions along with everyone else.'

'Management?' she frowned. 'Is that just you? Or do you have an entourage you take around with you?'

His expression darkened at the scorn in her tone. 'I have an entourage,' he bit out.

Her eyes widened. 'How many?'

He shrugged. 'Half a dozen highly trained people. They'll be here next week.'

'*Here* here, or just here in London?'

Rick's mouth quirked with amusement. 'Here here—they're already in London, they have been the last two weeks or so.'

'The same amount of time as you.'

'The same as me,' he nodded. 'They go everywhere that I go.'

'Everywhere?'

'Well, almost everywhere,' he chuckled throatily. 'I like my privacy at times like everyone else.'

'I can imagine,' she drawled. 'And who do "they" consist of?'

'A couple of secretaries, two personal assistants, a lawyer, and a P.R. man. Publicity is necessary some of the time,' he grimaced, 'but I want no part of it. Jack does a good job of keeping those sort of people off my back. I have a mobile office staff, we function from wherever we happen to be at the time, usually hotel rooms. It will make a nice change to have an office for a few weeks. I'm sure my people will appreciate it.'

'But there isn't room for another seven people here,'

Shanna protested. 'We barely have room for the staff we already have. Of course, there's the executive office Henry uses when he's here . . .'

'And this one,' Rick put in softly.

Her eyes widened as his words sank in. 'This one . . .?'

'Mm,' he smiled. 'You won't mind sharing with me, will you, Shanna? It seems a pity to throw someone else out of their office for the short time we'll be here. My two assistants, Jack and Peter, can take Henry's old office, Petra and Kate can move in next door with Gloria. Did you do anything about getting someone in to change this room?' he demanded abruptly.

Shanna was too stunned by his reorganising of his private staff into her offices to do more than nod. 'I have a man coming in this afternoon to discuss it.'

'Good girl,' he said appreciatively. 'Make sure you tone it down in here. Hell, I don't have to tell you, you've lived with this the last year,' he derided.

Henry looked puzzled. 'You're having this office redecorated?'

'Yes,' Rick drawled. 'Blue and white are my least favourite colours.'

'Oh, I see,' the other man nodded. 'I've always liked this office myself, but if you don't like it . . .'

'I thought maybe a restful green or brown,' Rick answered Henry, but he was looking at Shanna.

It was an instruction, she knew that. She also knew it was going to be nearly impossible to share an office with Rick for the next three months while she worked her notice.

'Make sure it's ready for Monday,' he added curtly.

'That's too soon—'

'I don't care what it takes,' he told her grimly. 'Triple time over the weekend, a bonus, whatever. But I want it changed before I come in here Monday.'

'I'll do my best,' she said tightly.

'That's good enough for me,' he nodded, his mouth twisted derisively. 'Well, I think that's all for now, don't you, Henry? We've taken up enough of Shanna's time for one morning, we mustn't keep her from her work any longer,' he taunted.

'The magazine has never run itself,' she told him tightly.

The two men stood up. 'Come to dinner tonight, Shanna,' Henry invited softly, taking one of her hands in his in silent apology for their argument on the telephone earlier this morning. 'I'd like to talk to you.'

She squeezed his hand. 'Not tonight,' she refused softly.

He glanced over at Rick and then back to Shanna again. 'You have a prior engagement,' he realised.

'No,' she answered tautly. 'I just don't feel—sociable today. I'd like to be alone tonight.' The last was said for Rick's sake as much as Henry's.

'Everyone needs to be alone sometimes, Henry,' Rick drawled, taking the hint.

Her brother nodded. 'I'll call you tomorrow, Shanna. Maybe we can see you some time over the weekend?'

'Maybe.' She was noncommittal, as she walked to the door with them.

'I'll see you on Monday morning, Shanna,' Rick told her with satisfaction. 'Bright and early.'

'The office opens at nine o'clock,' she said stiffly.

He nodded. 'I'll be here at eight. Have a good weekend, honey. I'll be away until late Sunday evening, so I won't see you until Monday morning,' he explained.

That suited her perfectly! A weekend free of him after two weeks of having him dog her every footstep would be a welcome relief. 'Eight o'clock,' she conceded agreeably.

He gave a grin, touching her cheek with gentle fingertips. 'I can hardly wait!'

She suffered his touch for several seconds before moving back, her smile tight. 'Neither can I.'

'I bet,' he mocked.

It took her several minutes to regain her composure after Henry and Rick had left. But at least she wasn't to have Rick's tormenting presence for the next five days; it had been worth putting up with his arrogant assumption that he could touch her just for that!

But her temples ached from just that one encounter. Three months, three *long* months——

Her eyes widened as her office door softly opened, tensing as Rick closed the door behind him. She stood up warily. 'Did you forget something?'

'Yes.' He advanced further into the room.

She frowned, looking about the tidy office. Nothing looked out of place. 'You forgot to tell me something?'

'Yes.' He stood in front of her now.

She stood her ground, her mouth suddenly dry as his dark gaze roamed slowly over her face, lingering on the parted softness of her lips. 'Yes?' she prompted nervously, feeling trapped, with her desk behind her and Rick in front of her. And he knew it, that knowledge was in the confidence of his black eyes.

'Yes,' he said again softly.

He was doing this deliberately! She should have known she couldn't escape for five days that easily. 'What is it?' she asked irritably.

'This,' he groaned, his head bending before his mouth captured hers, pulling her against the hardness of his body.

But that was the only similarity to the way he had

kissed her the night before; his lips were pleading for her response this time, tasting, cajoling, *tempting* . . .

'Put your arms around me,' he murmured against her lips, his hands linked at the base of her spine for closer contact with her, the hardness of his thighs telling her what the black glow of his eyes had already conveyed. 'I'm going to be away almost a week, honey,' he said softly. 'Surely one little kiss isn't going to hurt you?'

'I don't want to kiss you.' She strained away from him.

'I know that,' he said unconcernedly. 'But I'd hate to change my mind about going away. Now kiss me!' he instructed fiercely.

Shanna recognised a strength and determination more formidable than her own, giving a small sigh of capitulation as she put her arms about his neck and raised her face to his.

'*You* kiss *me*,' he reminded her throatily.

'I——'

'Kiss me, Shanna!' he ground out. 'And make sure I enjoy it!'

Her eyes were stormy as she raised her mouth to his, instantly knowing by his lack of co-operation that he wasn't going to make this easy for her. Damn him, he wanted a kiss—he was going to get one!

She arched her body against his, her breasts pressed against his chest as her hips moved slowly against him, her parted mouth moving erotically over his. With a deep groan his arms came about her like a vice, drawing her into him, every hard line of his body outlined against her, hiding none of his passionate response to her.

She pulled away, her gaze cold as she calmly registered the high flush to his cheeks, his eyes darkened even more with sexual excitement. 'You enjoyed it,' she told him icily, moving away as his arms dropped from about her.

His face tightened, his eyes narrowing as he breathed angrily. 'And all you enjoyed was knowing how you arouse me!' he rasped.

She sat down behind her desk. 'You didn't ask that I enjoy anything else. But then your sort never do.' She was deliberately insulting, hating the physical strength he had exerted over her to get his own way. 'Your own pleasure is all you're interested in.'

'I've never had any complaints,' he bit out.

'I'm sure you haven't,' she derided. 'But there's more to any relationship than being able to perform in bed. I'm sure no woman ever leaves your bed dissatisfied, Mr Dalmont, but it's still only a way of giving *you* pleasure. It would damage your ego, your self-esteem, if you couldn't tell yourself the woman had enjoyed it too. It's just another form of taking,' she dismissed scornfully.

'Was your husband a taker too?' he rasped. 'Is that why you're so familiar with the "type"?'

'Perry?' she gave him a startled look. 'No, Perry was not a taker,' she told him stiffly.

'Then why did your marriage fail?'

'It didn't fail!' Her eyes blazed.

'So your idea of a successful marriage is affairs on the side?' Rick taunted harshly, a white ring of tension about his mouth.

She swallowed hard, hating him more than ever in that moment. 'I've never had an affair,' she told him dully, knowing that hadn't been what he meant at all, but still too raw to accept the truth.

'No, but your husband had plenty.' Rick felt no such reluctance. 'Maybe you aren't a giver either.'

She looked at him with dull green eyes, the fire having left her face and body. 'Maybe I'm not,' she agreed evenly.

'Shanna——'

'I apologise if I was rude to you just now,' she told
him coolly. 'I had no right to say the things I did.'

'Of course you did, if you felt them. You're going
cold on me again,' he realised angrily. 'I really felt as if
I was getting through to you yesterday and this
morning, but now the cold Shanna is back,' he said
grimly. 'Is it because I mentioned your husband and
his affairs?'

'Not at all,' she dismissed distantly. 'I don't think it
was any secret then or now that Perry had—other
women.'

Rick's eyes were narrowed to black slits. 'But it still
hurts you, nonetheless.'

'Did you think it wouldn't?'

'I hoped not! It means you still love him,' he bit out
harshly.

'I've told you I do,' she nodded.

'But he's *dead*, Shanna. I'm alive, and I——'

'Want me,' she finished dully. 'Yes, I know. But
want and love aren't the same thing. Even if I didn't
still love Perry, I could never involve myself in so
selfish a relationship as wanting someone.' She shook
her head. 'I can never involve myself with *you*.'

'We'll see,' he told her fiercely. 'I have three months
of sharing this office with you, Shanna. And I'll break
you down, you'll see.'

He wouldn't break her down, she knew that. But
nevertheless, three months was a long time. It could
be a lifetime for her.

CHAPTER FOUR

SHANNA had prepared herself for another confrontation with Rick on Monday morning, but it wasn't he who entered her office at five to eight, it was another man, a man she didn't know, and yet one who was startlingly familiar.

Her gaze flew to the photograph of Perry that stood on her desk, the over-long blond hair and laughing blue eyes, the firm chin and lean capable body. The man standing in the doorway could have been his double!

'I haven't disturbed you, have I?' The man frowned his puzzlement at her suddenly pale face. 'I thought you told me to come in when I knocked.'

The first thing she realised was that his voice differed drastically from Perry's; his accent was distinctly American, the Bronx by the sound of it. And his nature looked as if it might be a little more intense than Perry's too, the laughter lines beside his eyes were not as plentiful. But the physical similarity was undeniable, and she couldn't seem to stop staring at him.

'Miss Logan?' he prompted concernedly.

'*Mrs* Logan,' Rick Dalmont corrected as he walked past the other man and into the room with a confidence that bordered on arrogance. He looked at Shanna with narrowed eyes, his formal appearance in a brown three-piece suit and cream shirt doing nothing to detract from the physical awareness of her in his eyes. 'What's the matter, Shanna?' he taunted. 'Seen a ghost?'

She gasped at the cruelty in his face, and tears welled up in her eyes, her throat moving convulsively.

'Come back later, Lance,' Rick turned to growl at the other man.

'But——'

'Later!' he rasped, moving purposefully around the desk towards Shanna.

She wasn't aware of the man called Lance moving, but she knew seconds later by the soft click of the door closing that he had indeed gone. She couldn't hold back the sobs any longer, and she buried her face in her hands as the tears flowed freely.

'Shanna——'

'You knew!' she flinched as Rick's hands touched her shoulders, glaring up at him. 'You knew that man—Lance looks like Perry!'

'Almost mirror image,' he nodded, and moved away, his hands thrust into his trousers pockets, his expression brooding. 'He's one of my assistants; his name is Lance Edwards. But I didn't know seeing him would affect you this badly.'

'Didn't you?' she choked her disbelief. 'I think you knew exactly how it would affect me—and that you're cruel enough to enjoy my reaction.'

He shook his head. 'When we first met I had no idea . . . Lance has worked for me for over ten years, Shanna, and until I saw that photograph of your husband on your desk last Monday I had no idea of the likeness between the two of them——'

'Perry's photograph was always in the newspapers when he was racing.' There was still accusation in her voice.

'And after,' Rick nodded. 'But I was usually too busy looking at the beautiful *Shanna* Logan to notice what her husband looked like.'

She blinked. 'You knew what I looked like before three weeks ago?'

He nodded again. 'And wanted you. But you

were married, were the socially popular Shanna Logan.'

'And I didn't have affairs.'

'No,' he acknowledged ruefully. 'So the grapevine informed me. Shanna, about Lance——'

'That was unforgivable,' she said bitterly. 'You could at least have warned me.'

'We didn't exactly part the best of friends last week, otherwise I might have done. It really did slip my mind, sweetheart——'

'Don't!' she shuddered at the endearment. 'Please don't.'

Anger blazed from his coal-black eyes. 'I'll call you what I damn well please,' he rasped.

'I hope that gives me the same privilege,' she snapped. 'Because I think you're a——'

'I think we both know your opinion of me,' he cut in harshly. 'It doesn't need any repeating, especially from such pretty lips.' His mouth twisted ruefully. 'I was going to ask if you'd missed me the last few days, but I think I already know the answer to that.'

'Yes!' she hissed, her mind still trying to assimilate the fact that there was a man in this building who could be Perry's double. The shock of seeing Lance still made her tremble.

Rick sat on the side of her desk. 'Aren't you even interested in where I've been?'

'Not particularly.'

He shrugged. 'I'll tell you anyway. I've been home to see my parents.'

'Your mother——'

'Is fine. Thanks,' he added warmly at her show of concern. 'I just hadn't been home for a couple of months, and as I'm an only child my mother tends to worry about me. At thirty-seven it's a little ridiculous, but I like to humour her.'

Yes, she could imagine that whatever else this man was he was a good son. He would have been brought up with all the Spanish sense of family unity and closeness, wouldn't shirk his duties as a son no matter what.

But she didn't want to like anything about this man, not even his respect and love for his family. He was cruel and barbaric, and she hated everything about him.

'What do you think of the office?' she prompted tautly.

He looked at the pale green and cream painted walls, even the carpet changed from deep blue to a pastel green. 'It looks fine,' he nodded.

'Is that all you can say?' she gasped. 'The men were here until ten o'clock last night finishing off, and all you can say is that it looks fine!'

He shrugged. 'There isn't a lot else that can be said about green and cream walls,' he derided.

'You were vocal enough about the blue and white!'

'Because I didn't like it.'

'I take it that means you do like the new colour scheme?'

'Oh, I get it,' he smiled. 'Yes, I like it very much, Shanna. You did a good job.'

She stiffened at his patronising tone. 'And I wasn't seeking praise from the master like all the other simpering women who adorn your life!' she snapped.

'What a nasty little tongue you have at times, my darling.' He bent forward, his face only inches away from hers. 'Careful I don't bite it off one of these days—or nights.'

She blushed at his implied intimacy. 'I had a desk moved in for you over there, Mr Dalmont,' she pointed to the large wooden desk that had been placed in front of the other large window in the room. 'Please use it.'

'Oh, I will.' But he made no effort to move.

'Then do so now!' Shanna snapped her agitation.

'In a minute,' he dismissed. 'Lance *isn't* Perry, Shanna, just remember that,' he warned softly. 'If you have to imagine anyone as your husband I'd rather it was me—with all the privileges that go with the role.'

'You're disgusting!'

'I'm staking a claim,' he corrected grimly. 'One you would be well advised to heed.'

'No one could ever take Perry's place!'

'Not even Lance?' he taunted softly.

She stood up noisily. 'No one! Now if you'll excuse me I——' she didn't get any further, for the door was flung open noisily, and a beautiful blonde woman of about thirty stood in the doorway, the light blue dress she wore clinging lovingly to her tall voluptuous curves, her shoulder-length fair hair softly waving and very feminine, her make-up heavy without being too much. She was a very attractive woman, if a very angry one at the moment. And Shanna had never seen her before, she was sure of that.

'Rick, I refuse to work in the same office as that moron Jack!' she burst out furiously, her beautiful face twisted in anger, her body moving in natural seduction as she came further into the room.

Rick sighed and stood up. 'Jack isn't a moron, and you know it. And I wish the two of you would settle your differences away from work!'

'We don't have any differences,' the woman snapped. 'At least, none that couldn't be solved if he left.'

'Or you did,' Rick pointed out softly.

'Oh, Rick, you don't mean that!' She moved up close to him, touching his cheeks with caressing fingers. 'What would you do without little old me?'

'I'd have harmony among my personal staff,' he

said derisively, removing her hand to hold her at arm's
length. 'I don't believe you've met Shanna Logan,' he
drawled, knowing very well that the two women had
never met before. 'Shanna, this is my other personal
assistant, Cindy Matthews. Cindy, this is the editor of
Fashion Lady, Shanna Logan,' he introduced
smoothly.

For some reason it had never occurred to her that
Rick's second assistant would be a woman. She didn't
know why it hadn't, women could definitely go as far
in business nowadays as men, and Rick Dalmont
would like women about him at all times. The
intimacy with which Cindy Matthews treated him
seemed to imply that their relationship didn't always
exist just on a business level. That definitely didn't
surprise her!

The other woman was looking at her with equally
speculative blue eyes. 'You aren't what I was
expecting,' she said bluntly. Another American!
Shanna had a feeling that all Rick's personal staff
would be.

She gave a smile; the other woman's directness
appealed to her. 'I could say the same about you,' she
drawled derisively.

Cindy returned the smile. 'You were expecting a
man, huh?'

'Yes,' she admitted.

'So was I when she came for her interview,' Rick
revealed dryly. 'She signed all her correspondence
with my New York office C. Matthews. I was a little
surprised when a woman turned up.'

'Admit it was more than a little,' Cindy taunted.

'All right,' he laughed. 'I was more than a little
surprised, I was astounded.'

'He doesn't like women working for him,' Cindy
confided to Shanna.

'Really?' she taunted. 'Now that does surprise me.'

'I think he finds them a distraction.'

'Then how did you get the job?' Shanna joined in the teasing, liking the fact that Rick was on the receiving end of the mockery for a change; she doubted it happened very often!

'Her qualifications were too good to pass up,' Rick drawled. 'Thirty-eight, twenty-four, thirty-four.' He laughed at Cindy's look of outrage. 'I'm right, aren't I?'

'You're the expert,' Cindy nodded. 'Now what are you going to do about my working conditions?'

'You know the rules, Cindy,' his own humour faded. 'You share with the boys as usual.'

'But you know how strained things are between Jack and me,' she pouted.

'I also know why,' he said grimly. 'I warned you about involvements like that in the beginning. It doesn't work in a close working relationship like the one we have.'

Shanna instantly revised her opinion of Rick being emotionally involved with the other woman. He wouldn't make one rule for his employees and another one for himself. If he disapproved of relationships between his employees then he wouldn't indulge in them himself either. Then why make her the exception? Because he had known from the first that she would never stay on and work for him!

'Perhaps Miss Matthews——'

'Cindy,' the other woman invited.

'Shanna,' she returned. 'Perhaps you would like to share an office with Jane Meakins, the assistant editor? I'm sure she wouldn't mind, and——'

'But I would,' Rick rasped. 'Cindy made her bed, and now she'll have to lie on it.'

'But not with Jack,' Cindy snapped.

He shrugged. 'I seem to recall you weren't saying that a week or so ago.'

'You're an unfeeling swine!' Cindy turned on her heel and slammed out of the room.

Shanna felt dismayed to have witnessed such a scene, knowing that Rick wasn't going to thank her for her interference either. She had only been trying to help, and—She gave him a sharp look as he began to chuckle.

'Don't look so worried,' he mocked lightly.

'But Cindy——'

'Knows damn well that she'll be sharing with Jane by tomorrow,' he mused.

'But you told her——'

'It's a little game Cindy and I play; I win the first round, but she always wins the battle. It's been that way ever since she came to work for me three years ago.' He shook his head. 'I think she lets me think I've won to save my pride.' He sighed. 'I guess I'd better go and talk to Jane. Unless you would prefer to do it?' he arched dark brows.

'No, thanks,' Shanna refused dryly. 'I wouldn't want to spoil your—game.'

'Shanna——'

'Besides,' she added mockingly, 'I have a feeling Jane would just love you to go into her office and see her. It will start her week off perfectly.'

His eyes were narrowed. 'What's that supposed to mean?'

'You must know that all the female staff on the magazine are half in love with you already,' she scorned, having heard nothing but speculation and admiration for Rick Dalmont for the remainder of the previous week.

'All except its editor!'

She nodded coolly. 'Don't feel too bad about that, Rick. You can't win them all.'

'I don't want them all,' he paused at the door, 'I want you. And I'm going to have you,' he told her confidently.

She glared at the closed door after he had left. He wasn't going to 'get' her at all—no one was. She took two tablets out of her handbag, swallowing them down, wondering if her nervous system was going to be able to take working with Rick.

She almost choked on the tablets as Gloria came into her office, her hand shaking as she put the glass of water down. 'Doesn't anyone knock any more?' she snapped irritably. 'People have been walking in and out of this office today as if it was a railway station!'

'Sorry,' Gloria said without remorse. 'I just arrived, and—Did I hear Rick Dalmont say he *wants* you?' Her eyes were wide with speculation.

Shanna drew in an angry breath, thinking fast. It was one thing for her to know Rick's intent, quite another for the whole of the staff of *Fashion Lady* to know it too. 'You only heard part of the conversation, Gloria,' she told her secretary calmly. 'You may as well know that I've handed in my resignation at *Fashion Lady*. Mr Dalmont was merely—merely trying to talk me out of it.'

'And did he?' Gloria gasped.

'No.'

'You're really leaving?' the other girl frowned.

'Yes.'

'But that's terrible! What is it, don't you like Mr Dalmont?' she asked avidly.

Much as she liked Gloria and valued her services as her secretary, she also knew the other girl was an incurable gossip. The fact that she was leaving *Fashion Lady* would be broadcast over the whole building by lunchtime, but she wanted no speculation as to the reason she was leaving. It was no one's business but her own.

'I like him very much,' she lied. 'I just have the offer of another, more interesting job.'

'Where?' Gloria asked interestedly.

'It's all a little delicate at the moment, Gloria,' she invented. 'I'd rather not talk about it yet.'

'Oh,' the other girl looked crestfallen. 'Well, we'll be sorry to see you go.'

'Yes.' Shanna held back her smile, sure that every female member of staff would prefer to see Rick Dalmont walking about the building than her. A month after she had gone these people would have trouble remembering her face. She couldn't blame them for that, the new owner was more important than old management.

She was hard at work when Rick came back to the office fifteen minutes later. She didn't look up, she didn't need to, she just knew it was him as if by instinct.

'Do you mind?'

She looked up slowly. 'Mind?' she frowned, her concentration on a fashion layout broken.

'If I smoke.' He held up a cheroot. He was seated behind his own desk, a huge file opened in front of him.

'No, go ahead,' she nodded, bending back to her work.

'Some people don't like the aroma.'

'Really?' He was surrounded by smoke when she glanced up at him this time.

'Mm, I suppose if you don't smoke yourself it can be unpleasant.'

'Yes,' she answered vaguely.

'Personally, I've always found the——'

'Rick, if we're to share this office you'll have to get on with your work and I'll have to do mine,' she told him in a carefully controlled voice. 'I don't mind if you smoke, I don't mind what you do, I just want to get on with checking this layout—Amy is waiting for it.'

His eyes narrowed through the smoke. 'I meant what I said earlier, Shanna,' he said softly. 'Lance may look like Perry, but he isn't him. And I'll never stand for you going out with him.'

'I have no desire to go out with him. As *I* told *you* earlier, no man could ever take Perry's place.'

'*This* man is going to,' Rick bit out grimly.

'I thought you didn't like to get involved,' she taunted.

'I don't. Three months will be long enough for me.'

'More than long enough for me.' She stood up. 'I have to go and see Amy in Fashion. I'll see you later.'

His mouth twisted. 'I don't intend going anywhere.'

Shanna swept past his desk and out of the room, her head high as she made her way to the Fashion Department, spending over an hour with Amy Roberts going over the latest fashion layout. She knew she was being more thorough than usual, malingering, not wanting to return to her own office. And this was only the first day!

'Hey, Shanna.'

She turned at the sound of that lighthearted voice, smiling as she recognised Cindy Matthews. 'Hello,' she returned softly.

Cindy walked down the corridor to join her, a friendly grin on her face. 'I just wanted to apologise for this morning.' She shrugged. 'Rick and I like to rile each other, but I guess I forgot we weren't alone.'

'It's all right—Rick explained.'

'I'll bet he did!' the other woman grimaced. 'He's a fantastic guy to work for, and most of the time we get on great together. But he really is mad about Jack and me.'

'You were friends?'

'A bit more than that,' Cindy admitted ruefully. 'It was a stupid thing to do, Rick told me the rules, but I couldn't resist the big ape.'

'Rick?' she taunted.

'Jack,' the other woman laughed. 'You could never call Rick an ape. He has style, from the top of his head to the tip of his toes.'

'And Jack doesn't?' she teased, reaffirming the fact that she liked this woman, liked her friendliness and her blunt way of speaking.

Cindy pulled a face. 'Oh, he has style—too much of it. He can't resist any pretty face that comes along. He was making a play for one of the secretaries here the last time I saw him.'

Shanna had the impression that the lighthearted words hid a wealth of pain. No matter how lightly Cindy dismissed Rick's P.R. man she liked him much more than she was willing to admit, maybe even loved him. She couldn't understand how any man could resist Cindy; she was beautiful, intelligent and witty. What more could any man want?

'But enough about Jack,' Cindy brushed him aside as if he weren't important. 'I really am sorry about this morning.'

'I told you, it doesn't matter,' Shanna assured her. 'Has Rick told you yet that you'll be sharing with Jane as from tomorrow?'

Cindy grinned. 'Not yet, but I guessed it. He'll just keep me waiting a while before he tells me.'

'Another part of the game?' she mocked.

'I suppose it is,' Cindy answered slowly. 'A game, I mean. But then most of life is, isn't it?'

'There seem to be more losers than winners.'

'Hey, that's cynical!' Cindy frowned.

Shanna shrugged. 'It's also the truth.' She gave a regretful smile. 'I'd better be getting back.'

'No, come along and meet the gang.' Cindy put a hand on her arm. 'They're all dying to meet the first woman ever to——' she broke off, biting down on her bottom lip.

Shanna raised dark brows. 'Ever to what?' she prompted softly.

The other woman grimaced. 'Me and my big mouth!'

'Ever to what?' Shanna repeated firmly.

Cindy sighed. 'Rick has been pretty impossible since he met you. We all figured it's because you turned him down.'

'How do you know his mood has been because of me? It could be some other woman——'

'No way,' Cindy shook her head confidently. 'He went to a party, met you, threw that bozo out of the hotel—Sorry,' she added ruefully. 'The bozo was Anna Kalder—the actress. At least, she thinks she is. She had cotton-wool between her ears. I don't know where Rick gets them from. All his women are beautiful, but a bit lacking in brains, you know.'

'Maybe he prefers them that way,' Shanna dismissed coolly, not at all interested in Rick Dalmont's 'women'.

'You disprove that idea,' Cindy grinned. 'A woman with brains and beauty at last!'

She returned the smile wryly. 'Too much brains to get involved with a man like Rick.'

'Mm, that's what we figured,' the other woman replied seriously. 'But he hasn't given up, has he? You have to admire his singlemindedness.'

'Believe me, Cindy,' she scorned, 'I don't have to admire anything about him—and I don't.'

Cindy whistled through her teeth. 'You just have to come and meet the others, they'll never believe it if I tell them.'

'Tell them what?' Shanna managed to ask as she was half dragged down the corridor.

'That you've managed to resist Rick this long because you really *don't* like him. He's had other women play hard to get,' she shrugged. 'But that's all it was—pretence. You're the genuine article.'

'I may be,' Shanna admitted. 'But I don't intend broadcasting the fact.'

'You won't have to.' Cindy stopped triumphantly outside the executive office Henry had always used in the past. 'Just to listen to you is enough.'

'Cindy——'

'Just come and meet everyone,' she persuaded. 'Rick should have introduced us all by now.' She grinned. 'You'll have to excuse him, sexual tension makes him forget his manners!'

She had opened her mouth to give a sharp retort when the office door opened unexpectedly, and the words froze on her lips as she gazed up at Lance Edwards, unable to believe even now how like Perry he was. She had persuaded herself the last two hours that she had blown the likeness up out of all proportion in her mind. But she hadn't—oh, she hadn't!

'Mrs Logan?' he frowned as she stared at him wordlessly.

'*Mrs?*' Cindy echoed in disbelief. 'Hey, you aren't married, are you?' she gasped.

'Widowed,' Shanna managed between stiff lips.

'Thank God for that,' the other woman sighed. 'Oh, not that your husband is dead,' she added hastily. 'I just thought for a moment that Rick had broken all his own rules and gone for a married woman.'

'Why don't you shut up, Cindy,' a man drawled from inside the room, 'before you stick your foot in your mouth any further.'

She turned blazing blue eyes on the man. 'Mind your own damned business!' she snapped. 'How was I supposed to know Shanna was married?'

'By making a few enquiries before you jumped in with both feet,' he taunted, tall and dark, very good-looking in an obviously muscular way, turning a seductive smile in Shanna's direction. 'You'll have to excuse Cindy, she never stops to think before she speaks.'

'Just because I don't nose into other people's lives——'

'It's my job to nose,' he returned tautly. 'And when I have to I hush up whatever Rick says I should.'

Shanna had listened to the exchange with growing awareness that this must be Rick's P.R. man Jack. 'And what did he tell you to hush up about me?' she asked tartly.

'I——'

'The whole thing,' Lance answered for the other man. 'Rick is very newsworthy, but he's deliberately kept your name out of the newspapers.'

She turned shadowed green eyes on the blond man. 'Why?'

'To protect you——'

'I don't need protecting,' she said sharply. 'And even if I did I wouldn't ask it of a man like Rick Dalmont.' She became aware of the sudden silence in the room once she had finished, and turned slowly to find Rick standing in the corridor behind her. 'Perhaps you would like to explain,' she said tautly.

'Gladly,' he nodded, his expression cold. 'If I knew what it was I had to explain.'

Nothing ever shook this man's confidence! Her mouth tightened angrily. 'Why everyone seems to assume that I'm your latest conquest,' she snapped. 'Someone whose name you're keeping out of the papers in connection with yours. Can you tell me why everyone thinks that?' she demanded.

'Do they?' he taunted.

'Obviously!'

'Perhaps we could talk about this later, Shanna,' he bit out softly, aware of their stunned audience even if she wasn't. 'In the privacy of your office.'

Did the others notice the slight emphasis on the word privacy? She certainly did, realising just what she had done. Her antipathy towards Rick should have been kept between the four walls of her office, not displayed in front of these people who had respected and worked for him for years. 'I'm sorry,' she said stiltedly. 'I—Excuse me,' and she turned and fled, ignoring Rick as he called her name.

She was behaving like a fool today, had decided to act so cool, and instead she had been stupid. Stupid, stupid, *stupid*! Rick certainly wouldn't let her get away with that, her excuse that seeing Lance Edwards this morning had unnerved her wouldn't make any difference to a man as hard as Rick Dalmont. And seeing Lance Edwards, his likeness to Perry *was* no excuse for her rudeness to Rick just now, rather she should be thanking him for keeping his interest in her *out* of the newspapers!

'Hey, are you all right?'

She looked up from her desk to find Cindy had followed her back to her office, coming in to close the door behind her.

'Rick sent me after you,' she explained gently as she came to stand at Shanna's side, her hand resting lightly on her shoulder in silent comfort.

Shanna swallowed hard. 'Rick did?'

Cindy smiled. 'Don't worry about what happened just now. Rick can take it. Believe me, this will all blow over in a few days.'

'Rick doesn't appear to me to be the forgiving type,' she grimaced.

Cindy shook her head. 'He cares about you, Shanna——'

'No! No, he doesn't. He——'

'Yes, Shanna,' Cindy insisted firmly. 'I should have guessed from the beginning, we all should. He doesn't usually give a damn about the publicity his lady-loves get when they're with him, and neither do they. But he's tried to keep you out of it from the beginning——'

'Because I'm not one of his lady-loves!'

'I know that,' Cindy sighed. 'We all know that—now. But I think we half guessed it already. He was only trying to help you, Shanna, to protect you.'

'But Shanna doesn't need protecting.' The man himself walked in, lacking none of the confidence that was a fundamental part of him. 'Do you, honey?' he derided.

Cindy looked away uncomfortably—an emotion Shanna felt sure was alien to the other woman. 'I—er—I'll get back to my office.'

'You do that,' Rick drawled pleasantly.

'To answer your question,' Shanna snapped once they were alone, 'I can take care of myself, from the press or anyone else.'

'And if you don't always need to?'

'Even then,' she nodded coolly. 'However,' she sighed, 'I do owe you an apology for any embarrassment I may have caused you just now. I forgot where I was for a moment.'

He raised dark brows. 'Apology accepted.'

'But unexpected,' she derided.

'Yes.'

She gave an unwilling smile at his bluntness. 'I don't mind admitting when I'm wrong.'

'Then have dinner with me tonight.'

'Implying that I've been wrong to refuse you in the past?' she mocked.

Rick grinned, his good humour seemingly restored. 'You learn fast, Shanna.'

'So my college professors always told me,' she nodded. 'They also taught us a sense of self-preservation, so if you don't mind I'll refuse your invitation to dinner.'

'Self-preservation?' he echoed softly. 'You make it sound as if you aren't as immune to me as you would like to be.'

She flushed, realising she should never give this man an advantage of any kind, not even a verbal one. 'It's just a figure of speech,' she dismissed abruptly.

'Nothing personal, huh?'

'Nothing,' she bit out. 'Rick, would you rather I moved next door with Gloria and your two secretaries come in here? I'm sure it can't be very convenient for you this way.'

'Maybe not,' he shrugged. 'But it sure is a hell of a lot more interesting. You won't change your mind about dinner?'

'No.'

'I'll see you later, then. I have a luncheon appointment in half an hour,' he explained. 'A failing airline I might be able to bail out.'

Her eyes widened. 'Don't you ever stop acquiring new businesses?'

'Nope,' he shrugged. 'I've found no viable substitute to that challenge yet. Maybe when I do I'll work and play a little slower.' He moved swiftly around her desk and kissed her hard on the mouth, a gleam of satisfaction in his eyes as he raised his head at her lack of resistance. 'You see, you're getting used to my kissing you. Pretty soon you'll be so used to it you won't even look surprised.'

'I doubt it,' she said tautly, indignation burning within her at his audacity.

'You will.' He straightened, moving to the door. 'By the way, I'm taking Lance with me, so don't get the idea that you can sneak back to his office once I've gone.'

She stiffened at his insinuating tone. 'I don't *sneak* anywhere in this building, Mr Dalmont. Until a few days ago, I ran it! As for going to that particular office again, Cindy thought I should be introduced to the rest of your staff, something you apparently didn't think of.'

He scowled at her intended rebuke. 'I've had other things on my mind.'

'Cindy had an idea about that too,' she taunted.

'I'll just bet she did!' His scowl deepened. 'That young woman is getting too big for her pants— trousers,' he amended in a slow drawl. 'Pants are men's shorts over here, aren't they?'

'I'm sure you know that they are.'

'Just checking.' His humour seemed to be back intact. 'I'll do the introductions when I—when Lance and I,' he corrected pointedly, 'get back from lunch. In the meantime, perhaps you could try and rub off a little of that frosty disdain you have in such abundance on Cindy. She really knows how to pick the wrong men. Jack is a great P.R. man, but as far as permanent relationships go he's no good,' he shook his head ruefully. 'Cindy's got to a stage in her life when she needs to settle down with one man, get married, have kids. Although don't tell her I told you that,' he grimaced. 'She thinks she's the original career woman.'

'There's nothing wrong in a woman having a career——'

'Not when that's what she wants, no,' he agreed.
'But Cindy's gone past that now, she needs more than
a career alone can give her.'

'She can't have marriage and a career?' Shanna
derided.

'She could,' he nodded, completely serious now, 'if
she didn't want kids too. But there's a lot of maternal
instinct inside Cindy just bursting to come out.'

'Are any of your personal staff married?' Shanna
queried mildly.

'They wouldn't be any good to me if they were,' he
answered instantly.

'That's an arrogant assumption——'

'It's a sensible one,' he corrected. 'No man—or
woman—can give me his best when he—or she,' he
derided again, 'is just longing to get back to his or her
spouse. I know damn well I wouldn't be able to.'

'And if you ever marry?'

'My wife will travel with me, of course,' he stated
with arrogance.

'The same couldn't apply to your staff?'

'We're a work force, not a marriage guidance
council! Which reminds me, I want to talk to you
about the magazine's problem page when I get back.'

Shanna frowned. 'But we don't have one.'

He nodded. 'That's what I want to talk to you
about. See you later, sweetheart.'

She glared at the closed door, for once the
endearment not bothering her. Only Rick Dalmont
could make such an enigmatic statement and then walk
out. *Fashion Lady* had never had a problem page, had
never needed one. And yet she had a feeling they were
going to get one.

CHAPTER FIVE

RICK was too busy to discuss anything when he got back late that afternoon. Talks on the airline had apparently progressed a further stage, and Rick was spending most of what was left of the afternoon with his lawyer, Peter Lacey, going through contract suggestions.

It was like watching a tornado at work. The two men pored over papers on Rick's desk, although Rick was definitely the more quickwitted of the two, showing he wasn't just a figurehead to Dalmont Industries but a very active member of it.

Just to watch and listen to his decisive and intricate dealings with the airline made Shanna feel tired, and it was with more than her usual relief that she packed up for the day. Her nape ached, her head throbbed, and what she needed most was a relaxing shower and a quiet dinner.

'Tired?'

She looked up to find Rick watching her unconscious kneading of her nape, his eyes narrowed. She instantly removed her hand. He hadn't paid any attention to her all afternoon and now he had to catch her in a moment of weakness! 'Of course not,' she denied stiltedly. 'I've just been bent over these layouts all afternoon.'

'Neck ache?' he persisted.

'Only a little,' she admitted grudgingly. 'Nothing a hot shower won't cure.'

He quirked dark brows, looking as immaculate and unruffled as he had first thing this morning. 'Sounds interesting,' he drawled.

Shanna pulled on the jacket of her navy blue suit, the crisp white blouse she wore underneath adding to her look of cool competence. 'There's nothing interesting about my taking a hot shower, Rick,' she told him briskly as she walked to the door. 'Goodnight,' and she swept from the room before he could come back with any smart retort. He seemed to have one for every occasion!

But her tiredness was a tangible thing, and instead of taking her shower after she had undressed and put on her robe she fell asleep on the bed. She hadn't meant to, she was invited to a friend's party this evening, and yet a short lie-down turned into a deep sleep that was only interrupted by the insistent ringing of the doorbell. By the time she had pulled herself up from the blankets of sleep that cocooned her the doorbell had stopped ringing, and she dropped back weakly against the pillows, shaking from the suddenness with which she had been woken.

'Shanna!' Rick rasped worriedly as he came striding into the room, sitting on the side of the bed as she struggled to sit up, grasping her shoulders painfully as she swayed weakly. 'What the hell is it?' he demanded, shaking her. 'Shanna, speak to me! Are you on something?' he grated roughly.

'On something?' She pushed her dark hair back out of her eyes. 'What—No,' she groaned in denial. 'No, of course not. I was tired, you know I was. I—What are you doing here?' She was coming fully awake now. 'How did you get in?'

'Your lock isn't very strong——'

'You broke in?' she gasped.

'No, I didn't *break* in,' he dismissed impatiently, standing up to thrust his hands into his trouser pockets, navy blue trousers that clung to the lean length of his thighs and legs, a lighter blue shirt fitting tautly over his chest and stomach. 'I told you, that lock is too fragile. A credit card and a little skill and I was in within seconds.'

'You broke in!' she accused.

'And what was I supposed to do?' He glared down at her, his eyes black. 'I could hear water running and no one answered the door when I rang. I knew you were tired, despite your denial earlier—you could have fallen asleep in the bath and drowned for all I knew!'

Only one thing he said made any sense to Shanna—or rather it *didn't* make sense. 'Water running?' she frowned her puzzlement.

'Yes. Can't you hear it?'

She could now, now that he had pointed it out. But where was it coming from? She didn't remember—'The shower . . .' she realised weakly.

Rick gave her an impatient glance before striding into the adjoining bathroom, and the sound of the water spray stopped seconds later. When he came back seconds later he just stood looking down at her.

Shanna moistened her lips, then straightened her robe, checking that the belt was fastened securely before she stood up, conscious of her nakedness beneath the green silky material even if Rick wasn't. Although she had a feeling he was more than aware of it as his gaze never left her as she moved about the room.

'You were asleep.' He was finally the one to speak. 'What was the shower doing on?'

Once again she moistened her lips with the tip of her tongue. 'I was going to take a shower, and then I—then I decided to take a nap first and shower later. I—I must have forgotten to turn off the water.' She omitted the most important part, about how weary she had suddenly felt after undressing, how she hadn't had the strength to step beneath the water she had been running, how she just had to lie down. She didn't tell Rick any of that, and she didn't intend telling anyone else of the feelings of weakness that had been increasing lately, how sometimes she couldn't even get out of bed in the morning. It was no one's business but her own; she owed no explanations to anyone.

'Do you often—forget to do things like that?'

'I—Sometimes,' she dismissed lightly.

'It doesn't sound like the Shanna Logan I know.'

She shrugged. 'I'm not at work now, Rick. I'm allowed to forget things in my own home. I was just waking up when you rang the doorbell. I would have been there to answer it——'

'But you couldn't get up,' Rick frowned. 'Are you always this tired when you get home from work?'

No, sometimes she was even tireder! 'No, of course not,' she snapped. 'Look, instead of questioning me would you mind telling me what you're doing here?'

'Dinner,' he stated bluntly.

She flushed angrily. 'But I told you——'

'That you wouldn't have dinner with me.'

'Will you stop putting words into my mouth and listen to me!' she snapped. 'I'm capable of speaking for myself.'

'I've noticed,' he drawled. 'But as you wouldn't have dinner with me I decided to come and have dinner with you.'

'I'm not going out to dinner, either with you or without you.'

'Now you're the one who isn't listening. I said I've come to have dinner *with* you.' He took his hands out of his pockets. 'Which is precisely what I intend doing. While you dress I'll get dinner.'

'Rick!' she stopped him at the door. 'Rick, I'm going out.'

'Not before you've eaten,' he shook his head. 'Then if you still want to go out I'll take you. Didn't you eat lunch, is that why you look so washed out?'

She drew in an angry breath. 'You certainly know how to flatter a woman!'

'You look terrible, Shanna——'

'I don't have my make-up on,' she snapped. 'Can I help it if you don't like the naked me?'

'Oh, I like the naked you, Shanna,' he took a threatening step towards her. 'What I can see I like very much.' His long sensitive hands framed each side of her face. 'I just don't like to see the shadows under these beautiful green eyes.' His thumbtips smoothed the dark circles beneath her eyes. 'And you're so pale. Sweetheart, you don't look well,' he frowned.

'I'm always pale when I wake up,' she excused herself abruptly. 'Just give me a few minutes and I'll put on my make-up and get dressed. I'll look fine then. But I don't have anything in for dinner, Rick, nothing I could give you anyway.'

'I brought it with me,' he dismissed. 'Hotels are okay when I'm away on business, but I get a little tired of restaurant food. I went shopping for steak and salad, cheesecake, wine, and——'

'*You* did?' she looked at him in disbelief. 'You went shopping in a supermarket?'

His mouth twisted. 'You can't see me doing that, eh?'

'No,' she answered truthfully.

'To tell you the truth, I've never done it before,' he shook his head. 'It was like a jungle.'

'I'm sure you're the first millionaire they ever had in their shop.' She couldn't help her humour.

'Shanna, let me cook you dinner,' his voice was husky. 'Then if you aren't still pale I'll take you wherever you want to go.'

'And stay with me,' she realised dryly.

'Of course,' he drawled. 'Privilege of the cook.'

Shanna stepped away from him, relieved when he made no effort to stop her. 'I only have your word for it that you can cook. You're right, I did miss lunch, and I need a good dinner, not a burnt offering,' she mocked him.

'Just wait and see,' he warned. 'You'll want me to cook for you again.'

'Not if you break in I won't.' She began to brush her hair. 'Do you realise I could have you arrested?'

'But you won't,' he said confidently.

'I'm still thinking about it!' His manner angered her.

'In that case,' he stepped over the frivolous green mule slippers she had taken off before lying down on the bed, coming determinedly towards her, 'I'd rather it was for something more interesting than opening that feeble lock.'

'Rick——'

'Shanna,' he taunted, taking the brush out of her hand before pulling her hard against him. 'You have the sexiest body I've ever seen,' he murmured throatily. 'Or touched. Or wanted. You're driving me insane, sweetheart,' he groaned before his mouth possessed hers.

She told herself afterwards that her defences had been down after her sleep, that she wasn't properly awake. Whatever her excuse, she responded to Rick Dalmont with an abandonment that later made her blush with shame.

But right now there was no thought for anything but Rick's mouth moving druggingly over hers, the heat of his body pressed against her, his hands roaming freely over her slender curves.

'God, how I've waited for this,' he groaned into her

Say Hello to Yesterday
Holly Weston had done it all alone.

She had raised her small son and worked her way up to features writer for a major newspaper. Still the bitterness of the the past seven years lingered.

She had been very young when she married Nick Falconer—but old enough to lose her heart completely when he left. Despite her success in her new life, her old one haunted her.

But it was over and done with—until an assignment in Greece brought her face to face with Nick, and all she was trying to forget....

Time of the Temptress
The game must be played his way!

Rebellion against a cushioned, controlled life had landed Eve Tarrant in Africa. Now only the tough mercenary Wade O'Mara stood between her and possible death in the wild, revolution-torn jungle.

But the real danger was Wade himself—he had made Eve aware of herself as a woman.

"I saved your neck, so you feel you owe me something," Wade said. "But you don't owe me a thing, Eve. Get away from me." She knew she could make him lose his head if she tried. But that wouldn't solve anything....

Your Romantic Adventure Starts Here.

Born Out of Love
It had to be coincidence!

Charlotte stared at the man through a mist of confusion. It was Logan. An older Logan, of course, but unmistakably the man who had ravaged her emotions and then abandoned her all those years ago.

She ought to feel angry. She ought to feel resentful and cheated. Instead, she was apprehensive—terrified at the complications he could create.

"We are not through, Charlotte," he told her flatly. "I sometimes think we haven't even begun."

Man's World
Kate was finished with love for good.

Kate's new boss, features editor Eliot Holman, might have devastating charms—but Kate couldn't care less, even if it was obvious that he was interested in her.

Everyone, including Eliot, thought Kate was grieving over the loss of her husband, Toby. She kept it a carefully guarded secret just how cruelly Toby had treated her and how terrified she was of trusting men again.

But Eliot refused to leave her alone, which only served to infuriate her. He was no different from any other man... or was he?

These FOUR free Harlequin Presents novels allow you to enter the world of romance, love and desire. As a member of the Harlequin Home Subscription Plan, you can continue to experience all the moods of love. You'll be inspired by moments so real...so moving...you won't want them to end. So start your own Harlequin Presents adventure by returning the reply card below. <u>DO IT TODAY!</u>

**EXTRA BONUS
MAIL YOUR ORDER
TODAY AND GET A
FREE TOTE BAG
FROM HARLEQUIN.**

throat, his mouth moving slowly down to the hollows at its base, his tongue tasting every silken inch.

Shanna trembled against him, the first sexual excitement she had known in a long time ripping through her body in a red-hot ache, and she made no demur when he swung her up in his arms to place her on the pale green silk bedspread, curving his lean length against her side as he continued to kiss her on the mouth.

His hands moved with deft movements to the single tie-fastening of her robe, untying the simple knot, parting the silky material to reveal her nakedness. 'Oh, God . . .' he murmured shakily, his own body leaping with desire as one of his hands moved tentatively up to cup her breast, his thumb moving with sure arousal over the deep red tip. With a groan his head lowered and his lips caught the nipple in pleasure-giving movements, his tongue soft and then hard in circular movements.

Shanna arched against him, a moan escaping her throat as he bit down erotically on the hardened nipple, sucking it deeper into his mouth, tugging gently. Her breathing was ragged as he continued to caress the other breast, the other nipple now caught between thumb and finger as he squeezed with just enough pressure to make her shudder with desire.

She was lost in a haze of passion and need as he parted her legs to move between her thighs, the roughness of his clothing abrasively pleasure-giving as he moved down her body with slow kisses of discovery and desire, lingering over her navel before moving down to the mound of her womanhood.

Shanna whimpered softly as she felt his lips and tongue there, shaking so badly now she was almost out of control, her breath coming in sobbing gasps.

Rick moved up beside her, frowning his concern.

'I'm not hurting you?' he asked gently, smoothing back her hair.

She swallowed hard, shaking her head. 'I just—It's been too long—It's too much for me!' she moistened her dry lips with the tip of her tongue. 'I'm not sure I'm ready for this.'

His eyes darkened even more, a deep enigmatic black as he gazed down at her for long timeless seconds. 'Then we'll wait until you are ready.' He spoke huskily, swinging his legs off the bed to stand up. 'You're looking pale again anyway. I think I should feed you, not make love to you.' He leant over to touch her cheek with a gentleness that brought tears to her eyes. 'Dinner in ten minutes,' he said briskly. 'Is that long enough for you to dress? If not, just stay as you are.'

She couldn't do that, they both knew that. Whatever had happened just now she had no control over it, knew that Rick had been the one in control from start to finish, and to stay in this robe would be an invitation to more of the same.

Ten minutes later she was dressed in a severe black dress, its high collar and loose style giving her a look of cool sophistication rather than flattering the perfection of her body, her make-up erasing the pale and tired appearance she had had when she woke up. Rick was in the kitchen when she joined him, and she withstood his searching gaze with cool challenge, determined not to blush or show embarrassment at the intimate discovery he had made of her body. Not in front of him anyway! Later, when she was alone, it would be a different matter.

'Can I do anything to help you?' she queried distantly.

Rick's mouth twisted. 'No, thanks, I'm over it now,' he taunted.

He was being deliberately provocative, and her mouth tightened. 'Dinner smells delicious.' She refused to be drawn into an intimate conversation with him, intending showing him that nothing had changed between them because of a few moments of weakness in his arms.

'Then let's hope it is,' he nodded, and turned back to the steaks.

'You didn't answer my question,' she prompted.

'What was it?' he derided.

'Would you like me to do anything?'

'Several things,' he drawled. 'But all of them are out of the question at the moment; the meal is almost ready.'

'If you're going to be rude I'll leave you to it!' she snapped, turning to walk out of the room.

Rick caught up with her in two strides, jerking her round to face him. His eyes glittered down at her. 'Don't try and pretend that what we just shared together didn't happen,' he grated. 'It happened, Shanna,' he told her grimly. 'I know, because I still ache for you in my gut!'

'Rick——'

'I let you go this time, Shanna, but next time I won't. You understand me?' He shook her slightly.

She swallowed hard. 'I understand.'

'As long as you do.' He thrust her away from him and returned to the grilling steaks.

They ate in silence, neither of them in the mood to break it. Shanna was too full of self-recrimination, and Rick, she felt sure, was kicking himself for turning down this golden opportunity he had had to make love to her. She was determined there wouldn't be a 'next time'.

'You're a very good cook,' she told him once they had cleared away.

'Thanks,' he nodded abruptly, enjoying one of his cheroots after their meal.

'Where did you learn to cook like that?'

'University. Shanna——'

'Which university did you go to?' she asked quickly.

'What the hell does that matter?' he rasped.

'I was just interested——'

'You were just avoiding my conversation, is what you were doing,' he bit out grimly, stubbing the cheroot out in the glass ashtray. 'I'm not going to be put back in that ice-box, Shanna,' he told her tautly. 'I made love to you an hour ago, and I'm not going to let either of us forget it.'

'It was a mistake——'

'It was beautiful,' he corrected harshly. 'It was better with you than with any other woman I've ever known.'

Her mouth twisted. 'That line is far from original, Rick,' she derided. 'We also know it's untrue.'

'Damn you, it's the truth!' he told her savagely, sitting forward. 'I'm not dealing in lines here, I'm dealing in sanity—*mine*. If you want to drive me out of my mind just keep saying no.'

'I intend to!'

'And I'll just keep showing you that you really mean yes! Damn it, Shanna, I know I said I wanted to take your husband's place——'

'For three months,' she scorned.

He gave an angry sigh. 'For any amount of time. I know now that isn't possible for any man, that your husband will always remain a part of you.'

'A part you aren't interested in!' Her eyes flashed.

'Not true.' He shook his head, coming down on the carpet in front of her chair and taking her hands in his. 'Tell me about him, Shanna, talk to me. Tell me what went wrong between you——'

'No!' she wrenched away from him. 'I don't intend discussing any aspect of my marriage with you, not the beginning or the end of it. I'm Perry's widow, that's all you need to know—or respect. But you don't respect widowhood, do you, Rick?' she scorned. 'You've shown that from the first.'

'I respect the living; the dead are exactly that— dead. No matter how long you show your love and loyalty to Perry, a month, a year, *ten* years, he'll still be exactly that—dead,' Rick said grimly. 'No amount of celibacy—or loneliness—can change that.'

'I remain celibate, and lonely, through choice,' she told him raggedly. 'You obviously can't be either. Why do you always have to be proving what a macho man you are?' she derided. 'And why are you afraid to be on your own occasionally?'

He was frowning darkly. 'I'm not macho, Shanna. I could be very gentle with you if you would let me close enough. And I'm often alone, people who spend a lot of their life in hotels usually are. The others, my secretaries and assistants, all go their own way when we leave the particular company we're working with at the time.'

'I've seen the "way" you go from the newspapers,' she dismissed hardly.

'You make me sound like a sex-hungry Romeo!'

She remained unflinching in the face of his anger. 'And aren't you?'

'I enjoy women, I've never made any secret of that, not since the first time when I was sixteen. But I only have a healthy sexual appetite, not the excessive one you're implying. If I were married it would be perfectly normal for me to make love to my wife three or four times a week, although I'm told that twice is the norm,' he derided. 'And it's possibly a lot higher than that when you first marry.

You would know more about that than I do,' he raised mocking brows.

Shanna flushed, her mouth tight. 'You're doing very well without any help from me.'

A grin flashed across his harsh features before he was once again serious. 'Well I, as a bachelor, do not make love three or four times a week. I haven't made love for over three weeks, now, for instance,' he added pointedly.

The blush stayed in her cheeks this time, knowing she was the reason for his abstinence; he was nothing if not singleminded, and his pursuit of her had definitely been that. 'Is that a record?' she scorned.

He drew in a harsh breath. 'As a matter of fact, yes! Does that give you satisfaction?'

'Your sex life doesn't interest me.' She turned away.

Rick straightened, looking down at her. 'It doesn't interest me much at the moment either, it's non-existent!'

'Maybe that will change tonight.' Her mouth twisted at his raised brows. 'I don't mean with me. If you come to the party with me now I'm sure there'll be plenty of women there only too happy to help you with your—little problem.'

'It isn't little.' He laughed at her indignant gasp. 'And my parents could tell you that a very stubborn child grew into a dogmatic man. I don't want any of the women at the party, Shanna.'

'You haven't even seen them yet!'

'And I'm not going to. Neither are you, for that matter.'

'What do you mean?' she frowned.

'I told you I would take you wherever you wanted to go if you didn't still look pale. You do, so you aren't going anywhere, except maybe to bed.'

'You——'

'Alone,' he drawled. 'To sleep. Now.'

'You can't order me about!' she gasped indignantly. 'If I want to go out I'll damn well go!'

'Try it,' he warned softly.

'Rick, I want to go out!'

He frowned at her near-desperation. 'Are you sure you aren't the one who's frightened of being alone? Shanna, what—Hell, are you going to faint?' he moved to grasp her arms as she swayed, her face paler than ever. 'Shanna?' he hissed as she leant weakly against him. 'What's wrong with you?' he rasped. 'Do you need a doctor?'

'No,' she dismissed through stiff lips. 'I—I think you're right, I need an early night. I've been overdoing it lately.'

Rick's arm about her waist supported her into the bedroom, his frown one of deep concern. 'It's all these damned parties you keep going to,' he said angrily. 'How can you expect to function properly when you go out every night and hold down a job in the day, especially one with the responsibilities yours has?'

'You do it,' she accused weakly, sitting down on the bed.

'I've built up an immunity over the years.' He pushed her hands away to pull her dress off her shoulders. 'From what I understand you've only been behaving this way since your husband died.' He put his arms around her to release the fastening of her bra. 'Calm down,' he snapped as she flinched. 'I'm putting you to bed, not raping you.'

'But I can undress myself——'

'And I can do it with much less effort.' He talked down her protests, laying her on the bed to remove the rest of her clothes, going over to the dressing-table to search through her drawers for a nightgown and coming back with a black lacy one. 'I'll be having fantasies about you all night,' he mocked gently as he pulled the garment over her head. 'Just for a change!' He stood her up to pull back the bedclothes and tuck her comfortably beneath the crisp sheets, sitting on the side of the bed to gently touch her cheek. 'You have to slow down, Shanna. The body, your body, can only take so much before it burns itself out. Heed the warnings, sweetheart, your tiredness, your weakness. If you don't you'll kill yourself.'

Sleep wouldn't be denied once he had left, and her mental decision to go to the party once she was alone became impossible as she knew she didn't even have the strength to get out of bed. Rick could have no idea how right he was. She was killing herself, slowly but surely . . .

There were no signs of tiredness about her as she entered her office the next morning, and she returned Rick's questioning greeting with cold politeness, wanting their relationship back on the strictly impersonal.

She put her burgundy-coloured briefcase on her desk-top and took out the notes she had been working on the previous evening.

Rick stood up to come over and lean on the side of her desk. 'How do you feel today?' he asked gruffly.

She looked up at him with cool green eyes. 'Just fine, thank you. Now yesterday you mentioned something about——'

'Shanna, it won't work,' he interrupted gently. 'I told you that last night. And the fantasies I had of you during the night tell me I didn't imagine one thing that happened between us in your apartment yesterday evening. I don't have that vivid an imagination!'

She swallowed hard. 'I can't work with you if you're going to constantly remind me of one lapse I had with you. I was tired, I wasn't thinking straight. Now could we talk about this problem page you mentioned yesterday?' She looked at him steadily.

For long breathless minutes he continued to look down at her, seemingly undecided about whether or not to take her lead. Finally he shrugged. 'You don't like the idea?' He straightened, every inch the businessman in his blue tailored suit and snowy white shirt.

'What makes you say that?'

'I think it was the way you pronounced "problem page",' he derided. 'You make it sound like two dirty words.'

'And isn't it?'

'A survey shows that the majority of women turn to the problem page in magazines first.'

'Whose survey?' she asked dryly.

'Mine. Oh, not personally,' he mocked. 'I had people out on the street doing it for me.'

'Where?'

He smiled. 'Central London. Satisfied?'

She shrugged. '*Fashion Lady* has always got along very well without a problem page.'

'All those women can't be wrong, Shanna.'

'Can't they?'

'No,' he shook his head decisively.

'*Fashion Lady* has always been above such things,' she dismissed.

'Then we'll just have to drag it down to my level, won't we?' he taunted abruptly. 'Because I intend to go ahead and have a problem page in the first issue of the magazine for next year.'

Her eyes sparkled with temper. 'Then why bother to tell me you wanted to talk about it?'

'Courtesy,' he dismissed. 'You are still the editor of *Fashion Lady*.'

'Not for too much longer!'

'Mm,' he nodded thoughtfully. 'Which reminds me, did you do anything about advertising for a replacement for you?'

'I've been in touch with an agency that specialises in such things. There's a couple of women who look quite promising.'

'I want to be in on the interviews.'

'Why?' she gasped. 'Don't you trust me, is that it?' Her tone was aggressive.

'You're being childish now——'

'I want to know why you feel you have to be present at interviews for prospective employees for my job,' she glared at him. 'I think I have a right to know that.'

'You have that right,' Rick nodded abruptly. 'And I have no objection to answering you. I want to be in on those interviews because I have to work with the woman who replaces you long after you're gone.'

'And forgotten,' she said tightly.

'You're never out of my mind, Shanna,' he told her throatily. 'And you know you aren't. Look, surely you can see the sense of what I'm saying?' He quirked dark brows.

'Of course,' she nodded stiltedly. 'As soon as the interviews are arranged I'll let you know. Unless you would like to do that too . . .?'

Rick gave an impatient sigh. 'No, you carry on. I can see there's going to be no reasoning with you today.' He held up his hands in dismissal.

'None at all.' Shanna stood up. 'Now if you'll excuse me, I have some work to do.'

It wasn't until she got out of the office and was walking along the corridor that she realised she had no idea where she was going! Heavens, she had allowed Rick to make her so angry that she had walked out of her own office!

'Hi, Shanna. How are you today?'

She turned thankfully at the sound of Cindy's cheery greeting. 'I'm fine,' she smiled. 'I was looking for you, actually,' she invented. 'You never did get round to those introductions yesterday, and Rick's too busy this morning for me to bother him with it.'

'Come right this way,' Cindy said lightly, as bright and bubbly as usual. 'I know the guys are all anxious to meet you.'

'The guys' turned out to be a pretty lighthearted bunch once they lost their initial awkwardness with her. Jack was exactly as she had thought he was, a flirt, Peter was very serious and quiet, and Lance was friendly without being familiar, obviously feeling she was still an unknown quantity.

'Do you enjoy the travel your work involves?' She tried to draw him into conversation, while Cindy and Jack were doing their usual bickering, and Peter was engrossed in the same papers he and Rick had been working on so intently the day before.

Lance shrugged; the two of them were in the sitting area of the office. 'It can get a little tiring, but for the most part I enjoy it. I enjoy working with and for Rick. He's a good boss.'

'Yes,' she agreed abruptly. 'I think I made—no, I *know* I made a fool of myself yesterday,' she told him ruefully. 'Rick and I don't really get on,' she chewed on her bottom lip. 'I think we both have strong personalities, and that doesn't make for working harmony.'

'But we all thought you and he—No, I guess not,' Lance drawled ruefully. 'Not after what you said yesterday. Does that mean you might be interested in a date with one of his assistants?'

'Cindy?' she taunted, not having expected this

invitation at all. It was a sure fact that Rick wouldn't approve!

Lance grinned, glancing over to where Cindy and Jack were still arguing. 'No,' he laughed, 'I wasn't thinking of Cindy.' He turned back to her, his blue eyes suddenly intense. 'Would you have dinner with me one evening, Shanna?'

'Rick wouldn't like it,' she warned him honestly.

He grimaced. 'I'm not asking Rick.'

She smiled. 'I meant he wouldn't like the two of us going out together.'

'I realise that. But I can handle it,' Lance told her quietly.

Shanna wasn't sure anyone could handle Rick's temper when he was aroused. And she also wasn't sure she should expose Lance Edwards to that. She had no doubt he was a nice man, a handsome one too, but she could never feel anything more than liking for him, despite his likeness to Perry.

'Rick explained your reaction to seeing me yesterday,' Lance spoke again as she didn't answer him. 'The reason you seemed upset.'

She frowned. 'What did he explain?'

'That I look a little like your husband. Hey, that's okay,' he soothed as she blanched. 'It doesn't bother me that you confused me with your husband for a while. I'm sure a lot of friendships have started on less than that.'

And Rick had just made certain that there couldn't even be friendship between Lance and herself. How dared he tell this man she reminded him of her husband? She knew how he dared, knew that he had told Lance that so that the other man would believe any interest she showed him was because of his likeness to Perry. And he had succeeded, damn him!

CHAPTER SIX

'YOU arrogant bastard!'

Shanna had remained in the executive office another half hour after turning down Lance's dinner invitation, and no one looking at her as she laughed and joked with the others could possibly have known of the anger boiling inside her.

It all came to the fore now as Rick looked up from the work on his desk with a surprised expression. 'How dare you tell Lance anything about me?' she stormed. 'What right do you have to go around telling men I only like them because they look like my husband?' she demanded furiously as he seemed to be digesting her words, taking a cheroot out of his case and slowly lighting it. 'Answer me!'

'You've spoken to Lance?' He did so.

'Obviously!'

He nodded. 'Obviously. Although I can't believe he said anything like what you're accusing me of.'

'So you didn't tell him he looks like Perry?' she scorned.

'Of course I told him that,' he rasped impatiently. 'I had to give him some sort of explanation for the way you behaved yesterday morning. Besides, the photograph on your desk only has to be seen for him to know that anyway.'

'So you deny telling him he looks like Perry because he would then think I only like him for that reason?' asked Shanna disbelievingly.

'Do you like him?' Rick snapped.

'As a matter of fact, yes!' She had found the other

man to be intelligent and interesting, and the longer she spoke to him the less she noticed any resemblance to Perry at all.

Rick stood up. 'Then I'm glad I told him what I did. And no, I don't deny I told him for exactly the reason you're accusing me of.' His expression was harsh. 'The situation between us is already confused enough without the addition of your going out with Lance.'

'I don't find it confusing at all,' she bit out. 'I don't like you, don't want to go out with you. And if I want to go out with Lance I will!'

Rick's eyes narrowed to black slits. 'Did he ask you?'

'Yes!'

'You won't go, Shanna,' he shook his head confidently, moving towards her determinedly.

She stood her ground defiantly. 'I will if I want to.' The fact that she didn't want to was none of his business.

'No!' His arms came about her like steel bands. 'Don't even think about it,' he warned raggedly. 'If you do I'll just have to do this a few times in front of Lance.' He claimed her mouth with fierce possession, bending her body into his. 'And if that doesn't work,' his eyes glittered like black opals as he raised his head, 'I'll just have to send him back to New York.'

'You wouldn't do that?' she gasped.

He nodded grimly. 'I'd do it, Shanna—believe me. Oh, I wouldn't fire him, he's too good a man for that, I'd just send him back to my head office there.'

That would be almost as bad for Lance, she knew that. The other man was very proud of his position as Rick's personal assistant; to send him back to America, in disgrace almost, would really injure his pride.

'You really are a bastard,' she told Rick with feeling.

He nodded cool acknowledgment of the fact, his mouth tight. 'If by that you mean I stake my territory and fight off anyone who comes near my property, then yes, I'm a barbarian.'

'I'm not your property. And you don't fight clean!'

'I fight with any weapons available to me,' he shrugged.

'But a man's career——'

'Is in your hands,' he drawled coldly. 'I've told you what the consequences will be if you go out with him; you know the penalty he will pay.'

'That isn't fair!' she sighed her frustration.

'Life rarely is,' he dismissed unconcernedly. 'Why not give up and go out with me, Shanna? I'll not let any other man touch you.'

'There must be some men in London that you can't get to,' she snapped.

He smiled, holding her easily in his arms as she struggled to be free. 'If there are I'll find a way, be sure of that.' His arms tightened about her. 'You're mine, Shanna, and the sooner you accept that the better.' His smile became a mocking grin. 'You'll see, I'm much easier to handle when I'm not consumed by sexual tension. And since meeting you I've known nothing else!'

'Don't expect me to do anything about that,' she told him tautly. 'Not even to get you out of my life will I go to bed with you.'

His mouth tightened. 'Not for that reason, no. Because it wouldn't get me out of your life—the opposite, I would think. I'd want to take it all over, Shanna, all your thoughts, all your smiles, your every waking moment. I'd entwine myself in your life so much you would feel haunted by me.'

'I do now!'

'As they say in the movies, "You ain't seen nothing yet, baby",' he mocked. 'At least at the moment I allow you to go home alone.'

'Oh? And who was the man who broke into my apartment last night? I'm having a new lock put on the door today, by the way,' she told him moodily. 'I don't like the idea of you being able to walk in any time you choose to do so.'

'Honey, I've just finished explaining to you that I would never leave if I had the *choice*,' he derided. 'But I'm waiting to be invited before I stay with you.'

'You'll wait for ever!'

'I don't think so.' His mouth twisted. 'I don't have that much patience. My parents would be amazed at the change you've made in me.'

'I'm sure it's only a temporary thing,' she scorned. 'Now will you kindly let me go?'

'You know the price.'

'And you accused me of being childish!' she flared at him.

'You were being at the time.'

'As you are now!' she snapped.

Rick gave a wolfish grin. 'I'm being far from childish, Shanna, I'm being *very* adult.' He curved her body more comfortably into his. 'What's one little kiss?'

'Between friends?' she scoffed.

'I never wanted to be your friend, sweetheart. Lover sounds much more—desirable.'

'If only I found you that way—desirable, I mean.'

'I've warned you about that tongue of yours, Shanna,' he rasped.

'I would think, I've had more opportunity to bite yours off than vice versa!'

He gave a deep frown of exasperation. 'You would try the patience of a saint. And as we both know, I'm far from being that,' he mocked her scornful look. 'You can imagine that my patience is almost non-existent. Now give me that sweet mouth of yours so that we can get on with our work.'

'Sweet, Rick?' she derided the description.

'When it isn't spouting abuse and insulting me,' he nodded with a taunting smile.

With a resigned shrug Shanna raised her mouth to his; she certainly never got anywhere by fighting with this man. Her arms moved up about his neck, fitting into the curve of his shoulder as he deepened and lengthened the kiss. She opened her lips to him, allowing him to search the warm cavern of her mouth for several seconds before she bit down, just hard enough to prove her point.

Rick was chuckling as he raised his head, releasing her with a light tap on the nose. 'You see, you do know how to play, after all.'

'Not by your rules,' she shook her head.

'You won't go out with me tonight?' He looked at her with narrowed eyes.

'No.'

'Okay,' he shrugged.

She eyed him suspiciously as he went back to sit behind his desk. He was accepting her refusal very calmly today—too calmly. Somehow she distrusted him more when he was this malleable. He was up to something, she didn't know what, but it gave her an uneasy feeling nonetheless. But there was no way he could interfere with her plans for tonight; she wasn't even going to be at home if he should call.

She knew the reason for his smugness all afternoon as soon as she walked into the lounge of Henry and Janice's London home; Rick was the only other apparent guest! They had worked in harmony for most of the day, had even joked together on a couple of occasions, and not once had he mentioned the fact that he was going to be at Henry's tonight too. And she knew damn well he had known she was going to be here, knew it by mockery in his dark eyes as he greeted her now.

'You made it okay, sweetheart,' he drawled softly, but loud enough for the other couple to hear and speculate at his intimacy. 'She's such an independent lady,' he turned to smile at Henry and Janice. 'I offered to bring her out here tonight, but she insisted on driving herself.' His arm moved about her shoulders in easy familiarity. 'Didn't I, honey?' he taunted.

He had too, she knew now that this had been where he was inviting her. How he must have been laughing at her all day, just knowing that her refusal meant nothing, that he was going to see her anyway. She had the feeling that Rick Dalmont was moving in for the kill step by stealthy step—and she was slowly running out of fight!

'Yes, Rick,' she agreed dully, and her head started to pound.

'Don't feel too bad, honey,' he grinned down at her as he sensed victory. 'You can drive me home instead; I came by cab again.'

'That seems to be a habit of yours,' she said sharply.

'Only when I know I have you to drive me home.'

She moved out of the arc of his arm, moving to kiss first Janice and then Henry on the cheek, handing to Janice the flowers that she had bought for her. 'You forgot to mention that Rick would be here tonight,' she looked at them both reproachfully.

'We thought you'd come together,' Henry dismissed.

She could guess the reason they had thought that

only too well, Rick's handiwork again. 'Is anyone else coming?' she asked brightly.

'No, it's just the four of us,' Janice smiled. 'I'll just go and check on dinner.'

'Are Peter and Susan asleep yet?' Shanna asked.

'If they are it will be the first time they ever have been before eight-thirty in the evening,' her sister-in-law laughed softly. 'I put them to bed at seven-thirty every night and they never go to sleep until at least nine o'clock,' she explained to Rick.

'They're great kids,' the doting father told him. 'But I don't know where they get their energy from.'

'Certainly not from you,' Shanna mocked her brother as he slouched in a chair.

'Could I go with you to see them?' Rick requested softly.

She turned to him in surprise. 'Wouldn't you rather stay and talk to Henry? I'm only going in to say goodnight to them.'

'Would it disturb them if I came with you?'

'Janice?' she looked questioningly at the other woman.

Her sister-in-law shrugged. 'They'll probably welcome the diversion. No offence to you, Rick,' she laughed, 'but my children welcome any excuse to evade going to sleep.'

'No offence taken,' he grinned, suddenly looking boyish. 'I used to do the same thing when I was a kid.'

'It's hardly the same thing,' Shanna dismissed derisively.

He quirked dark brows. 'Oh?'

'I'm sure your nanny always gave in to you. Janice takes care of her children herself.'

'My mother took care of me too,' he said tautly.

'Really?'

'Yes—really,' he bit out. 'She grew up in a strict

Spanish household, where the children were brought up by the family and not by strangers.'

'Why don't you take Rick upstairs with you?' Henry broke the tension. 'Otherwise dinner will be ready, and they'll both be asleep afterwards.'

'Would you like to come this way?' Shanna invited stiffly, and the two of them walked up the stairs together in silence. 'I'm sorry,' she sighed as they reached Susan's bedroom door, 'I had no right to be rude about the way you were brought up.' She put a hand to her temple. 'I just didn't expect to see you here tonight.'

'I know,' he said softly, moving her hand to replace it with his own, gently massaging her tension away. 'And I didn't tell you because I thought you would cancel.'

'I probably would have done,' she acknowledged wearily.

Rick sighed at the admission. 'Does your head ache?'

'Not really. I'm just tired.'

'Again?'

'It's been another long day,' she stiffened.

'Mm,' he nodded. 'I had no idea being an editor of a magazine like *Fashion Lady* was so time-consuming. Do you usually eat lunch at your desk?'

'Usually,' she acknowledged abruptly.

'Does Jane help you enough? It seems to me——'

'I didn't come here tonight to talk about work, Rick, but to forget about it for a few hours,' she cut in firmly. 'But just for the record, Jane does more than her fair share of the work. Now let's go and see Peter and Susan before Janice calls us down for dinner.'

As Janice had predicted, both children welcomed this diversion to going to sleep, looking angelic with their newly washed golden hair and matching blue pyjamas. Rick was surprisingly good with them, not talking down to them as some adults did, but treating them as equals. He was even prevailed upon to read them another fairy-story before they tucked them up in bed.

Shanna bent over to kiss both children goodnight, not at all surprised when Susan and Peter demanded a kiss from Rick too. He accepted this as the privilege it was, wishing them a softly spoken goodnight before joining Shanna in the hallway.

'They liked you,' she told him on the way back to the lounge.

'I liked them too,' he said gruffly. 'They're beautiful children.'

'Yes.' She smiled, feeling more relaxed with him after spending time with the children.

He frowned down at her. 'You never had children with Perry?'

She stiffened with the unexpectedness of the question. 'There never seemed to be the time.'

'Didn't he like children?'

'Very much,' she frowned. 'He always got on very well with Peter and Susan.'

'Did you plan to have children with him?'

'Yes,' she said abruptly. 'We discussed having them several times. It just—never happened.'

'I'm glad.'

She gasped. 'Why?' she breathed.

'Because I'm not sure I'm selfless enough to cope with your having another man's child,' he admitted reluctantly.

Shanna drew in a ragged breath. 'You don't have to *cope* with anything, not me or my non-existent child.'

'Don't I?' Rick looked down at her as if he were seeing her for the first time. 'I think I've underestimated you, Shanna Logan.'

She had no chance to answer him, as Janice announced dinner at that moment, and the four of them enjoyed a leisurely meal together. Rick was his usual charming self, and yet as the evening progressed she noticed he was quieter than usual, his conversation lacking the usual innuendoes for her, the easy familiarity with which he normally treated her now replaced by cool politeness; even the discussion about the changes in *Fashion Lady* was conducted in a businesslike way.

'So Shanna finally got her way about that,' said Henry when Rick told him of the introduction of a problem page.

'Did she?' Rick returned noncommittally, his gaze narrowed on her flushed and guilty face.

'She suggested it herself at the beginning of the year,' her brother explained guilelessly. 'But I thought that *Fashion Lady* didn't need one, that it——'

'Got along okay without it,' Rick finished in a slow drawl.

'Exactly,' Henry nodded, warming to his subject, not noticing the way Shanna was cringing as he progressed. 'Shanna even had a survey taken, to see how the public felt about it.'

'Really?' Rick drawled, looking at Shanna with enigmatic eyes. 'Where did you do your survey, Shanna?'

She looked back at him in stubborn silence, wishing she could have foreseen this conversation and averted it. It was true, she had put forward the idea of a problem page to Henry several months ago, and had done the same research on it then that Rick seemed to have done now—and Henry had turned it down without thought. It hadn't been part of his policy.

'Shanna?' he prompted now. 'Rick was talking to you.'

'Sorry,' she blinked. 'What was the question?' she delayed.

'Where did you do your survey?' Rick answered her this time.

'Central London,' she murmured.

'Sorry?' he quirked dark brows.

'Central London,' she said more strongly. 'It showed that the majority of the women we asked turn to the problem page first,' she told him before he asked.

'I see,' he nodded.

Shanna was relieved when Henry changed the subject, although she doubted she had heard the last of it from Rick. Strangely enough he was silent on the drive back to his hotel, so she decided to tackle the problem herself.

'The arguments I used today against the problem page were Henry's,' she told him quietly, driving him this time, with no protest from him, something she was sure he hadn't noticed, since he seemed preoccupied with thoughts of his own. 'The ones he used against me, I mean,' she added.

'So I gathered,' Rick said dryly. 'But you're really in favour of the idea?'

'Yes.'

'Then maybe you wouldn't mind interviewing some applicants for that job too? I was going to ask Cindy, but . . .' he shrugged dismissively.

'Would you like to be present?' she mocked.

'Not this time,' he shook his head. 'Just make sure she has the qualifications to deal with any letters that might come her way. Some of the answers I've read in other magazines—in the course of my research, of course——'

'Of course,' she drawled.

'Well, you don't think I read them through choice?'

he scorned. 'The mess people seem to make of their lives . . .! Still, they seem to help some people, and that's what matters. But some of the replies I've read in other magazines have been enough to make the person concerned go out and throw themselves off the nearest bridge!'

'I'll make sure that she—or he—is highly qualified,' she nodded agreement. 'It wouldn't do the magazine's reputation any good if someone sued us.'

'It wouldn't do the person any good either if they were dead!'

'No,' she sighed.

Rick lapsed into silence again, resting his head back against the leather upholstery.

'Tired?' Shanna prompted softly.

'No.' He didn't even open his eyes.

'Would you like to come to my apartment for a nightcap?' she heard herself offer, then her breath constricted in her throat as she realised what she had said. She didn't want Rick in her home, so why on earth had she invited him there? What on earth was *wrong* with her! 'A—a coffee or something?' she added awkwardly.

Cool black eyes stared at her in the gloom of the car; Rick's thoughts were as enigmatic as his expression. 'Coffee last thing at night keeps me awake—or do you want that?'

She gasped. 'I——'

'Forget it, Shanna,' he rasped. 'I didn't mean to say that. And I'll take a rain-check on the coffee. Thanks anyway.'

It wasn't the answer she had been expecting, she had thought Rick would jump at the chance to spend a little more time with her, especially alone at her home. What game was he playing now? Because his behaviour had to be part of the game, his game. What was it, the 'play uninterested' routine to spark her interest in him? Because if that was the case he was going to be out of luck once again; nothing would spark her interest in the playboy he was.

She dropped him off at his hotel, acknowledging his terse goodnight with a cheery one of her own. If he thought to disconcert her with his sudden coldness he was going to be disappointed!

Rick didn't act as if he were trying to do anything to her the rest of the week, ignoring her existence most of the time, almost snapping her head off at others. When the two women came for the interviews for her job on Friday she had no idea what to expect from him; his mood was volcanic.

'The first one was too young,' he dismissed. 'The second one was too involved in her marriage.'

'*Too involved in her marriage?*' Shanna echoed incredulously. 'How can anyone be too involved in a marriage?'

'She was,' he stated flatly. 'The editor of *Fashion Lady* has to put the magazine first.'

'Then why wasn't Stephanie Simms suitable?' she frowned. 'I know she was a little young, but I was only twenty-four when I took over.'

'You had inside help.'

Her mouth tightened at the insult. 'Henry wouldn't have given me the job if he didn't consider me capable. And as for Leslie Adams, I was married, and it didn't affect my efficiency.'

'You can't give the job to both of them.' Rick sat behind his own desk, and the room was filled with smoke from his cheroots; he had been smoking a lot of them lately, she noticed.

'I don't want to do that,' she said impatiently. 'I'm just pointing out that your reasons for turning them down are invalid, as both of them were applicable to me a year ago. The magazine hasn't suffered at my hands.'

'Granted,' he nodded. 'But I stand by my opinion of Leslie Adams. Did you see the way she hesitated when I asked if she intended having children?'

'Well, it was a personal question——'

'It was a valid one from any prospective employer. I believe Mrs Adams does intend having children, no matter what she said to the contrary, and I think she intends having them soon.'

'Then why bother to try for this job?' Shanna derided.

'Why not?' he shrugged. 'It would be something to tell her children when they're grown up.'

'I think you're being unfair to her. And Stephanie Simms' age shouldn't be a black mark against her either. Someone has to give her her chance.'

'Maybe when she's older,' he dismissed callously.

'Her qualifications are excellent.' Shanna had no idea why she was defending the other girl so heatedly. It was true that Stephanie Simms did have excellent qualifications, and equally good references from her last two employers, but she hadn't really liked the other girl, finding her efforts to flirt with Rick too obvious.

'I noticed,' he drawled, his thoughts obviously running along the same lines, his smile mocking. 'Miss Simms should go far.'

'But not here?'

'No.'

'I'm sure if you called her she would be pleased to convince you otherwise,' she said waspishly.

'No doubt.'

Her mouth tightened at his calm acceptance of the other woman's attraction to him. 'You don't sound surprised,' she snapped.

Rick shrugged his broad shoulders beneath the grey fitted jacket and snowy white shirt. 'I don't believe she made any secret of her method of getting to the top.'

'Then maybe you should give her a call.'

'Maybe I will,' he nodded, his eyes narrowed.

'That should be nice for you!'

'It probably would be. Now can we get back to the subject of your replacement?'

'Of course,' she answered abruptly. 'Maybe it would be better if you chose her yourself? If the decision had been left to me I would have taken on Leslie Adams.'

'So might I—if I hadn't already found someone.'

'Already found——?' Shanna stood up angrily and went over to stand in front of his desk, leaning over it as she glared down at him. 'You already have someone, and yet you still put those two women through a needless interview, acted as it they really had a chance of getting the job?' She was breathing hard in her agitation.

'You misunderstood me,' he told her calmly, lighting yet another cheroot. 'I didn't say I had already given the job to someone——'

'You mean it isn't a little surprise for one of your women?' she scorned.

He surveyed her coolly through the smoke. 'Not many of my "women" would be interested in this sort of work, Shanna.'

'How nice for them!'

'Perhaps,' he said without interest. 'And it wasn't until I saw our only two qualified applicants that I considered a third alternative.'

'Yes?'

'Cindy.'

'Cindy?' she echoed in a bewildered voice, her anger fading. Cindy?

'Yes.' Rick stood up, moving around the desk to

pace the room. 'The idea has been bouncing around in my head for a week now. She's capable of it, with training from you, and I think it could be what she needs to take her mind off Jack.'

Shanna had sat down on the edge of the desk in surprise. Cindy? It had never occurred to her to even consider the other woman. Cindy knew the world of business, had a superb sense of fashion herself, had been very interested in the running of the magazine the last week; Shanna had spent hours with the other women explaining different aspects of running the magazine. Yes, she had no doubt Cindy could do the job, that she would be very good at it. But would she want it? She voiced her doubts to Rick.

'It's what I think she needs,' he said arrogantly.

'Another way of getting her to settle down?' she scorned.

'She's hardly likely to find the right man moving around the world with me,' he replied seriously. 'I'm convinced the only reason she got involved with Jack was because he happened to be available at the time. Here in London she might have a chance of finding the right man for her.'

'Why don't *you* marry her, then you can both be happy!'

'I don't appreciate your humour, Shanna,' he bit out grimly.

'I suppose to you marriage must seem amusing,' she said bitterly.

He stubbed his cheroot out in the ashtray with vicious movements. 'It doesn't seem amusing at all!' he told her savagely. 'Not at all!' He strode across the room and slammed out of the door.

The door opened again a few seconds later, and Petra, one of Rick's secretaries, looked in at Shanna anxiously. 'Is everything all right? Rick looked a little—explosive,' she grimaced; she was a pretty girl in her early twenties, another American, as Shanna had thought she would be.

'Rick never looks a *little* explosive,' Shanna derided shakily. 'He was very much so. And I'm fine, thanks.'

'Sure?'

'Yes,' she smiled, not sure at all. She hadn't expected Rick to slam out like that, had never known him to react so strongly to one of her taunts before. But then he had been acting strangely all week; he was not the Rick Dalmont she thought she knew at all.

He didn't come back to the office for the rest of the afternoon, and as he had made no definite decision about offering Cindy the job as editor Shanna didn't mention it to the other woman when she came to the office late afternoon. No doubt it was something Rick would rather discuss with his assistant in private.

She went to a party that evening, and also one on Saturday evening, but as on the last four nights she saw nothing of Rick. He had suddenly stopped haunting her every movement, and was no longer there every time she looked round. The natural assumption to make was that he had found another woman to chase, that he had probably caught her, and that he had finally lost interest in her, Shanna.

The photograph of him in the Sunday newspapers walking into *the* club of the moment on Friday evening, with *the* model of the moment, Carrie, seemed to confirm that. Strange, she wasn't as relieved by his change of attention as she had thought she would be . . .

CHAPTER SEVEN

THERE wasn't much evidence of the new woman in his life doing much to improve Rick's temper when he came in on Monday morning, sending out cutting barbs to everyone he came into contact with, from Shanna to the innocuous Peter Lacey.

'I see the boss is back on form,' Cindy said dryly as she joined Shanna in her office for a sandwich lunch—after having made sure Rick had already left the office for his own lunch!

'Mm?' Shanna replied vaguely, preoccupied with her own thoughts.

'Here,' Cindy turned the pages on the newspaper Shanna had been reading so that she could see the photograph of Rick with an Italian film star, the dark-haired beauty clinging to his arm in open adoration. 'She isn't the same one he was photographed with on Friday.' She raised her brows pointedly.

'Or the one he went to lunch with just now,' Shanna said quietly.

Cindy's brows went even higher. 'He had a woman call for him here?'

'Yes.' She didn't elaborate on the fact that it had unsettled her to see the way the red-haired woman threw herself into Rick's arms, her pouting mouth clinging to his provocatively as he stood up to greet her. Shanna had recognised the woman as a television announcer, known for her glamour as much as her brains. And she obviously knew Rick intimately.

'Then he is back on form,' Cindy grimaced. 'I suppose it was too good to last. It's usually like this,' she explained at Shanna's questioning look. 'But this time I thought—Well, it's made a nice change not to keep falling over his women,' she amended awkwardly.

'It's all right, Cindy,' Shanna smiled. 'I had no doubt that Rick's interest in me would be fleeting. It only lasted as long as it did because to him I was the unobtainable. You see now why I wasn't obtainable. The last thing I need is an affair!'

'Why not?'

'Why?' she frowned. 'Because—well, because——'

'Rick's usually very good with his ladies, and as you aren't into permanent relationships either . . .'

Shanna had become good friends with Cindy over the last week, really liked the other woman, and she knew the liking was reciprocated. She had talked openly with Cindy, told her of her reluctance ever to marry again. 'I'm not "into" any sort of relationship, Cindy, you know that,' she said impatiently. 'Least of all becoming one of Rick Dalmont's numerous "ladies".'

'No one is asking,' rasped his gravel and honey voice as he came forcefully into the room, looking at them both coldly as they blushed guiltily. 'I don't care to have my private life discussed at some lunchtime gossip,' he snapped icily. 'What goes on in my life outside of this office is my affair,' he continued abruptly, 'and no one else's. Do you understand?'

'Yes,' Cindy mumbled, for once having no cheeky come-back.

He turned cold black eyes on Shanna. 'Both of you?' he prompted with soft menace.

She resented being treated like a child. He might intimidate Cindy, but he didn't frighten her, not in the least. 'You overheard a private conversation between Cindy and myself, not gossip——'

'A conversation about my personal life,' he bit out grimly.

'But not gossip,' she insisted.

'I disagree. Cindy, don't you have some work to do?' he glared at her in challenge.

They all knew that Cindy had at least another twenty minutes of her lunch-break left, and yet the other woman nodded, collecting up her things and leaving without a backward glance, just relieved to have got off so lightly.

'You're a bullying——' Shanna began.

'I'm in no mood for your insults today, Shanna,' he rasped dismissively. 'One more word and you're going to find your employment terminated right now!'

She stiffened, her own anger rising to meet his. 'Nothing would please me more!'

'I'm aware of that.' His mouth twisted. 'Which is precisely the reason I want you to get out of here now.'

'My pleasure!' She picked up her bag in preparation to leave.

'Only this office, Shanna,' he warned softly. 'Don't leave the building.'

She looked ready to explode. No one, *no one* had ever spoken to her in this way before. 'You wanted me to leave, so I'm leaving——'

'Not the building, Shanna,' he repeated, a smile to his lips now, the anger having faded to be replaced by taunting humour. 'I believe you've been looking for another job?' he added softly.

She wasn't deceived by his mild tone; she recognised the threat behind the words—and resented them. 'You wouldn't dare——'

'Wouldn't dare what?' he taunted.

'There's no way you could stop me getting another job,' she told him with haughty disdain.

'No? There's the question of your references. I believe prospective employers are very big on that sort of thing over here?'

'You wouldn't . . .?'

'If you leave now I can only assume that you've broken your contract, that you quit. I don't believe I have to give you references in the circumstances.'

She swallowed hard, hating him in that moment. 'You bastard!' she snapped coldly.

He gave a cool inclination of his head. 'Repetitious, but said from the heart. Now get out of here,' he ordered harshly.

'Didn't it work out?' she scorned as she reached the door. 'Your lunchtime bedmate?' she explained at his look of query.

Rick's mouth quirked. 'Samantha is very—accommodating.' He sat down. 'Ask Cindy to come and see me, will you?'

Shanna held in her gasp of indignation with effort. Who did he think he was talking to! She was the editor here, not some messenger girl. She wouldn't run his errands for him——

'Something wrong?' He arched mocking brows at her as she still stood in the doorway.

'Not a damned thing!' She slammed out of the room with suppressed violence. She wouldn't let him force her into leaving by ordering her around!

Lord, what a ridiculous situation! A couple of weeks ago she would have liked nothing better than to be able to just walk out of here, and now that Rick had challenged her to do just that she couldn't do it. He knew she needed his references, damn him, that no one would employ her, even as an errand girl, without her references. And only she knew how badly she needed a job, how she needed to keep busy all the time.

Rick pushed her to her limits over the next few days, making her run needless messages for him, talking to her in cold clipped tones when he bothered to talk to her at all, waiting for her to answer the telephone whenever it rang, whether it was on her desk or his. The atmosphere was so tense and uncomfortable that by Wednesday evening Shanna was at breaking point. The telephone rang on Rick's desk just as she was pulling on her jacket to leave, and by the sixth ring she knew he had no intention of answering it.

She snatched up the receiver, her hand over the mouthpiece. 'What did your last servant die of, Rick?' she snapped.

'It certainly wasn't kindness,' he drawled unconcernedly.

'I can vouch for that! Rick Dalmont's office,' she cooed sweetly into the receiver, glaring at Rick with dislike at the same time.

'Rick, please,' purred a throaty voice.

'It's for you.' Shanna thrust the receiver at him. 'And that's the last call I take from one of your women!' She seemed to have been doing nothing else the last three days!

'Jealous, Shanna?' he mocked, eyeing her challengingly.

'Go to hell!'

'I'm more likely to know heaven in Delia's arms,' he taunted. 'It is Delia, isn't it?'

'She didn't give a name,' Shanna bit out scornfully.

'Hello,' he spoke into the mouthpiece, his black gaze never leaving Shanna as she walked proudly over to the door. 'Yes, Delia,' there was mockery in his gaze now.

'Goodnight—Mr Dalmont,' Shanna told him curtly.

'Shanna?' he stopped her, his hand over the mouthpiece.

She stiffened. 'Yes?'

'You should try it some time,' he drawled. 'It does wonders for tension.'

She could feel the hot colour entering her cheeks. 'Maybe when you get your mind out of the bedroom, Mr Dalmont, you'll realise there's more to life than bedding as many women as you can!' She watched in amazement as he slowly put the receiver down and stood up to come towards her threateningly. 'I—Delia—She——'

'She'll call back,' he said grimly.

'How nice to be so confident!' she scorned, to hide her real nervousness.

'You should be less so,' he told her harshly, his fingers biting into her arm. 'My mind isn't in the bedroom at the moment, Shanna,' he rasped. 'It's envisaging how much pleasure I would get from putting my hands around that pretty little neck of yours and squeezing until no more sharp barbs could come from those delectable lips.'

She swallowed hard, looking up at him with wide eyes. 'I—I——'

'Frightened, Shanna?' he taunted hardly. 'So you damn well should be!' He flung her away from him with little regard for the fact that she struck her hip painfully on the door-handle. 'Go home, Shanna,' he added almost wearily.

'Rick——'

'I have a telephone call to make,' he bit out.

'Delia?'

'Who else?' he taunted, already dialling the number, turning his back on her as he sat on the side of his desk. 'Delia? Sorry, baby, my—assistant cut us off. Yes, it is hard to get qualified help nowadays,' he answered with humour. 'Now, about tonight——'

Shanna had heard enough, quietly closing the door

behind her as she left, leaning weakly back against it. It had been a strain working with Rick the last three days, with his desire turning to a need to punish. She wasn't sure how much more she could take.

It took all her will power to get out of bed and go to her office the next morning, dreading another day of Rick's unwarranted cruelty. She had even stopped going out in the evenings now so that she had enough strength to spar with him during the day. Even so, this constant battle of wills was sapping her strength, and she could feel the danger signals closing in on her.

Rick's desk was empty when she got in promptly at nine o'clock, and as he was usually in long before her this was surprising. There was no briefcase or papers on the desk to tell her he had even been in at all.

Cindy came into the office at nine-fifteen, her usual good humour not having suffered from Rick's temper this week. That was the one consolation to Shanna—Rick's bad temper wasn't directed only at her, although working with him as closely as she did she seemed to get the brunt of it.

'I don't think he's in yet,' she told the other woman with a smile.

'I know,' Cindy nodded. 'Did Rick tell you he's suggested I be editor here once you've left?' She came straight to the point in her usual straightforward manner.

'Yes.' Shanna's smile didn't waver. 'He said you're going to think about it.'

'I am,' the other girl frowned. 'I'm not sure I'm cut out to stay in one place.'

'Rick thinks you are.'

'And what do you think?'

'I think you are too,' Shanna nodded. 'We've worked together on a couple of things since you've been here, and I think you have a feel for this job. Besides, Rick will be here to help you for a while.'

'You don't mind?'

She stiffened. 'What Rick does is nothing to do with me.'

'I didn't mean that part,' Cindy chided. 'I meant, do you mind my being offered your job?'

'But it isn't my job—I resigned.'

'You don't regret it?'

'Not at all,' Shanna replied truthfully, knowing she couldn't continue working for Rick.

'Because of Rick?' Cindy guessed.

'Partly——'

'Mainly,' the other woman corrected.

'Perhaps,' she admitted.

'He's been such a bear lately,' Cindy frowned. 'I don't know what's wrong with him.'

'Well, it certainly isn't frustration any more,' Shanna derided. 'But it looks as if I shall be spared his temper today,' she looked pointedly at his empty desk. 'Delia must have proved as interesting as he thought she would.'

'And who is Delia?' Cindy frowned.

'The woman he was seeing last night.'

'Oh, her,' Cindy dismissed callously. 'I don't think she was interesting at all—he was back at the hotel by ten-thirty.'

That surprised her; she had been sure, by the way Rick spoke to Delia on the telephone, that he had intended it to be an all-night date. 'Are you sure he was alone?'

'Very much so,' Cindy said dryly. 'And in a lousy mood too. He had us all running around in circles last night about this airline deal.'

Shanna knew that Rick was going through with the acquisition of the airline, had gathered that much from conversations of his she had overheard. But she couldn't imagine what he could do to further its progress at eleven o'clock at night! She said as much to Cindy.

'Like I said,' Cindy grimaced, 'we were running about in circles. No one was available that time of night.'

'He must have been turned down,' Shanna taunted.

'By never-say-no Delia?' Cindy mocked. 'You've got to be kidding! If anyone said no it was Rick. He probably started to feel ill last night and wasn't in the mood.'

'Ill?' Shanna repeated in a puzzled voice.

'Oh, damn,' Cindy said impatiently. 'I came in here to tell you Rick won't be in today because he's sick and then I got sidetracked.'

Shanna shook her head, wondering at the sudden fear that clutched at her. 'What's wrong with him?'

'The doctor says——'

'Doctor?' she echoed sharply. 'He's bad enough to need a doctor?'

'Hey, calm down,' Cindy soothed. 'He only has the 'flu, not the Black Death!'

''Flu?' Shanna repeated with some relief. 'What did the doctor say?' She refused to question herself about her concern for a man she was supposed to hate.

'Bed rest and plenty of fluids.'

'And Rick meekly agreed?' She somehow couldn't envisage him doing that.

'Not meekly, no,' Cindy laughed. 'But as he's feeling too weak to get out of bed he didn't have much choice.'

'And the fluids?'

Cindy shrugged. 'The hotel will provide them.'

Shanna frowned. 'He's on his own?'

'Well, he didn't call for Delia or one of the other women he's seen this week, if that's what you mean,' Cindy derided.

She sighed. 'Do you think he's well enough to be left on his own?'

'Well, after he told us all to get out I'm sure as hell not going to volunteer to stay with him. He's more unbearable than usual!'

Shanna telephoned Rick's hotel once Cindy had left, only to be told that 'Mr Dalmont is not taking any calls'. Sleep would be the best thing for him, she decided, if he felt as ill as Cindy had implied he did— and yet as the day progressed she couldn't help worrying if he were all right. A hotel suite wasn't the best place to feel ill, and no one else seemed particularly concerned about him; all his personal staff were at work at the magazine as usual. She didn't doubt Cindy's word that Rick had told them to leave him alone—he would be impossible when weakened by illness!—but she wasn't sure it was good for him. What if he collapsed? What if the 'flu turned to something more serious?

It was no good telling herself that she had no need to worry about someone who treated her as badly as Rick did—she *was* worried, and there was nothing she could do about it.

Just as there was nothing she could do when she found she had driven to Rick's hotel that evening after she finished work. She convinced herself that as she was here she might as well go in and see how he was.

There was no answer to her knock on his suite door, but when she tried the door-handle it opened. All was quiet inside; the lounge was tidy enough, as was the first bedroom she tried. The second bedroom was a different matter! Crumpled tissues littered the floor and bedside cabinet, an empty jug and glass stood on top of the latter, clothes were scattered on the floor around the bed, as if Rick had only just managed to undress before collapsing on the bed. And it was there that he lay, the bedclothes lying badly crumpled about him, the dark growth of a day's beard very noticeable against the other pallor of his face, his eyes were closed, his breathing ragged and irregular.

He looked terrible, much worse than she had envisaged, and whether he wanted her here or not—and she was sure he didn't!—she wasn't leaving until she was sure he should be left alone. He didn't even look as if he were conscious!

'Rick?'

Heavy lids were instantly raised, cool black eyes glittering feveredly at her in recognition. 'What the hell are you doing here?' he bit out savagely, all the honey gone from his voice, only the gravel remaining.

'Nice welcome,' she said lightly, making some effort to straighten the bedclothes. 'These sheets are damp!' she frowned down at him.

'What did you expect?' he groaned weakly as he made an effort to sit up, dropping back against the pillows, his hair clinging damply to his forehead. 'I'm sweating like a——'

'I can see that,' she cut him off before he became crudely blunt. 'Well, you can't lie in damp sheets,' she told him briskly, picking up the telephone to begin dialling.

'What are you doing?' Rick glared at her, but he didn't have enough strength to do more than that.

'Calling for fresh sheets. What did you have in the jug?'

'Lime-juice. But——'

'Room service?' Shanna said haughtily as someone came on the line. For the next few minutes she gave instructions as to what she wanted sent up to Rick's suite, allowing no time for them to question her authority in turning their hotel upsidedown. After all, if Rick could afford to stay in a suite like this then he deserved the best service available too!

'Very efficient, Mrs Logan,' Rick drawled as she rang off. 'Except that I have no intention of getting out of this bed.'

'You——' she broke off her angry tirade as she saw the lack of real fight in him, the way he lay back weakly against the pillows, almost as white as the bed-linen itself. 'You'll feel better afterwards, Rick,' she soothed, and sat on the side of the bed, noticing how clammy his skin looked. 'Have you had your temperature taken?' she frowned, touching his forehead with the back of her hand, surprised at how hot he felt.

'A hundred and one,' he growled, his throat obviously troubling him too as he began to cough. 'God . . .!' he groaned weakly when he could catch his breath.

'Indeed,' she said dryly, standing up as a knock sounded on the door. 'I won't be long,' she promised, opening the door to admit an army of hotel staff as they brought in the things she had requested. 'Thank you,' she said warmly once everything had been deposited in the lounge.

'Will that be all for Mr Dalmont, madam?' One of the men lingered as the others left.

'Could you get this filled out?' she asked sweetly, handing him the prescription she had found amongst the clutter on Rick's cabinet. 'Mr Dalmont needs the medication as soon as possible.' She gave the man a glowing smile, handing him a large tip.

He glanced down at the money in his hand, his eyes widening appreciatively. 'Thank you, madam. I'll see to it myself.'

She had thought he might—no doubt he would expect another healthy tip when he brought the medication up to the suite too!

'Why didn't you get the prescription filled out?' she demanded of Rick as she took the fresh juice into his bedroom.

He opened his eyes with a weary sigh. 'Why do you keep doing that?' He put a hand up to his temple as it obviously ached. 'I feel like I want to die, and every time I fall asleep you come in and wake me up! Why don't you get the hell out of here and leave me alone?' he rasped.

'Maybe you would feel better if you'd taken the medicine the doctor prescribed for you,' Shanna told him without sympathy, beginning to strip the blankets from the bed.

Rick made a grab for them as his bare chest was revealed. 'There was no one to get it for me, and I didn't fancy struggling down to the chemists myself,' he taunted.

'According to Cindy you threw everyone out,' she said in a preoccupied voice, continuing to strip the bed.

'I didn't want anyone fussing around me,' he glowered at her, clutching at the sheet as she would have removed that too. 'Will you just stop what you're doing and——'

'Rick, don't be such a baby,' she sighed. 'I'm only——'

'I don't have any clothes on, for God's sake!' he rasped, glaring at her furiously, his face pale with the effort it cost him to move at all.

She hesitated for only a fraction of a second before she pulled off the last sheet, throwing it to one side. 'You think that bothers me?' she dismissed with only the slightest tremor in her voice. 'You aren't the first naked man I've ever seen.' She said the words confidently enough, and yet she couldn't quite bring herself to look at him, very conscious of his deeply tanned body lying on the snowy white sheet, of the blatant masculinity of that body.

'I'm aware of that,' he said icily. 'And ordinarily I wouldn't mind your seeing me,' he taunted as she blushed. 'But at the moment sex is the last thing on my mind!'

'It never even entered mine!' She turned back to him from folding the sheet, and her breath caught in her throat as she forced herself to look down at him dispassionately. He had a truly magnificent body, lean and muscled, covered with a fine dark hair that grew in wiry abundance over his chest and down over the flat planes of his stomach.

'I'm cold,' he muttered as she made no further move, mesmerised by the male beauty of him.

'I'm sorry.' She was galvanised into action, hoping he didn't notice her blushes in his own discomfort. 'Do you have a robe?'

'In the bathroom,' he nodded. 'But——'

She didn't wait to hear any more of his objections, but went to get the silky black robe. It smelt of his aftershave and the cheroots he smoked, and for a moment she was tempted to bury her face in its silkiness. Then she berated herself for her stupidity. She wasn't interested in this man, she *wasn't*!

She had hardened herself against the intimacy of the situation by the time she got back to the bedroom, and helped him into the robe and into a chair while she stripped off what remained of the bedclothes and began to remake it with fresh linen.

Rick lay back against the chair. 'You didn't have to do this,' he muttered ungratefully.

'And who else would do it?' She glanced round at him, hurrying in her task as she saw how much paler he had gone now that he was out of bed. 'Does Delia intend coming round later?'

'Heaven forbid!' he scowled.

'That's what I thought,' she said dryly. 'Now can you just sit there while I give you a wash and shave— or do you want to get back into bed while I do it?' She turned from making the bed.

'I'm going back to bed. And you *aren't* washing and shaving me anywhere!'

'Like to bet on it?' she mocked.

Rick glared at her belligerently. 'You think I'd let you anywhere near me with a razor?'

Shanna smiled. 'You are taking a risk, I'll admit that, especially after your nastiness the last few days. But I'm quite good with a man's razor; I used to shave Perry all the time after his first accident when he was confined to bed for a couple of months.'

'I'm sure he loved that!' Rick scorned.

A shutter came down over her expression. 'No, he hated it,' she said dully. 'But it did make him feel better, and it will you too.' She went into the lounge to get the bowl she had requested, hating herself for letting anything Rick said get to her.

It wasn't too difficult to find his shaving things, and armed with a bowl of warm water, his toiletries and towels, she went back into the bedroom. Rick had somehow managed to get himself from the chair back into the bed, lying sideways across it where he had fallen, and he now felt too ill to move.

A knock on the door took her out into the hallway briefly, to take the medicine from the effusive porter before hurrying back to Rick. He had to start taking the medication he had been given, and now.

Blazing black eyes glared at her as she gently shook him awake. 'Will you stop doing that!' he snapped. 'I want to sleep, damn you!'

'I know that, and in a minute you can. Take this.' She handed him the small plastic cup that came with the medicine, the correct dosage poured into it. She stood over him while he swallowed it down, knowing by the grimace he gave afterwards that it tasted as awful as it smelt. 'Now help me get you up the bed and on to the pillows. I don't think you should be lying flat like that,' she frowned as he collapsed back into his prone position.

'I didn't intend lying flat,' he scowled as with her help he moved up the bed. 'I just seemed to—to fall that way.' Once again he closed his eyes.

Shanna knew exactly how weak and helpless he was feeling. 'Flu sounded innocuous enough, when really it knocked you for six—even someone as capable and self-sufficient as Rick Dalmont! How he must hate her seeing him like this!

His eyes flew open as he felt her untying the belt on his robe. 'I thought I told you I'm not in the mood,' he sneered nastily.

'You did,' she confirmed briskly, determined not to fight with him any more; she would be taking an unfair advantage of him if she did, he was obviously in no condition to fight anyone. 'Don't be difficult, Rick, please. I'm taking your robe off so that I can wash you.'

'I don't need—Oh, to hell with it, woman, do what you please! You know damn well I can't stop you.'

She finally managed to get the robe off him, and the blanket bath she gave him was as efficient as any trained nurse could have done, knowing that despite his denial of needing the wash it was making him feel better. He was even helping her a little towards the end.

'Something else you learnt when Perry was ill?' he taunted as she pulled the bedclothes back over his nakedness.

'Yes.' She didn't rise to the taunt.

'What a devoted wife you were!'

'Yes.'

He gave an angry sigh. 'You can leave now.'

She knew he hoped to anger her by his dismissive tone, but she could be as stubborn as he when she had to be. 'Not until I've shaved you.'

'I——'

'You look like an escaped convict at the moment,' she spoke over his objection. 'I pity the poor women who wake up beside you in the mornings,' she added cheerfully.

Rick scowled at her. 'I usually shave morning and night; last night I didn't feel like it.'

'The shave or the woman?' she mocked, ducking into the bathroom before he could come back with an angry retort.

'Either,' he replied grimly when she came back with his razor. 'Be careful with that, won't you?' He shuddered as she came towards him.

Shanna laughed at how really worried he looked. 'Don't worry, you'll still be as handsome, even with only one ear!'

'Thanks!'

'Mm,' she smiled. 'But while I think about it, it isn't wise to leave your suite door open,' she told him sternly. 'Anyone could have walked in.'

'Anyone did,' he growled.

She moved the razor over the hardness of his jaw firmly but with care, making sure there wasn't even one little nick in the skin that he could complain about.

He didn't complain at all when she had finished; he didn't say a word—because he had fallen asleep! So much for wondering if she was going to cut his throat.

Shanna stood back to survey her handiwork. Rick certainly looked a lot better than when she had arrived an hour earlier, with his hair neatly combed, his face freshly shaved and the sweat bathed from his body, his bed newly made. He also seemed to be breathing easier, although she had a feeling the medicine might have a lot to do with that. She made sure the lime-juice was in easy reach for him when he woke up; he was sure to feel thirsty then.

She was just in the process of pulling on her jacket ready to leave when the door opened unannounced and Cindy stood transfixed in the doorway.

'Shanna!' she finally managed, slowly.

'Er—Hello.' Shanna moistened her lips awkwardly. 'I called round to see how Rick was, and then I——'

'Hey, you don't have to explain yourself to me,' Cindy dismissed lightly, closing the door behind her. 'I just came to see how he is myself, but I'm sure he preferred you to be his ministering angel.'

'Not so you'd notice,' she grimaced. 'He's asleep now, though. Look, Cindy, this isn't the way it seems. Rick and I——'

'It's none of my business,' the other woman assured her. 'How is he?'

'Not too good, but he wouldn't thank any of us for staying with him. I think I've left everything he needs within reaching distance. Cindy, about——'

'Please, no explanations. It's none of my business, remember?'

'But——'

'Look, you get on home, I'll keep a check on him tonight. You look tired yourself,' Cindy frowned.

She was tired, very much so. She also had the feeling that Cindy had gained completely the wrong impression about her being here in Rick's suite. And she wasn't giving her the chance to explain herself either.

CHAPTER EIGHT

She told herself over and over again that her feelings of anxiety for Rick were not necessary, that he had plenty of other people available to worry over him. And yet did he? He wouldn't allow anyone close to him, and although he was friends with the members of his entourage, he wasn't emotionally close to them, and the same could be said for his women, even the ones he had been seeing this last week.

Consequently she found herself worrying about him constantly during the night, telling herself she would feel the same about anyone who felt ill and was so far away from home. She even called the hotel again towards midnight, only to be told that Mr Dalmont still wasn't taking calls. After Cindy's erroneous assumption of earlier she was loath to call the other woman for fear of furthering her wrong impression any more.

She was up early and in the office long before everyone else, and yet she couldn't concentrate on her work. She kept seeing Rick as he had been yesterday when she arrived at his hotel, and somehow that thought disturbed her.

When Cindy came into her office just after nine she was ready to pack up and go to the hotel and see Rick. What Cindy had to tell her didn't change that decision; it just confirmed it.

'He threw us all out again,' Cindy grimaced. 'He threw me out last night too.'

Just because Rick had told her to go it didn't mean Cindy had had to do just that! But she didn't say anything reproachful to the other woman. 'How did he look?' she asked instead.

'Not quite as awful as yesterday—but almost. I've decided to give this job a try, by the way,' Cindy added thoughtfully.

'That's nice,' Shanna replied in a preoccupied voice. Cindy shrugged. 'I might as well. It's pure hell working with Jack since we broke up.'

'I'm sure you'll be a success,' Shanna smiled vaguely.

'Let's hope so.' Cindy walked back to the door. 'Rick doesn't bet on losers.'

Shanna tidied her desk as soon as she was alone, locking up to go and tell Gloria she was leaving for the morning at least, not sure whether she would be back in at all today. Gloria raised questioning brows, but Shanna didn't feel like satisfying that curiosity. She didn't even like admitting to herself that she was going to Rick's hotel to see for herself exactly how he was.

Once again the suite door opened when she tried the handle, and she was frowning as she walked into the bedroom. Rick was asleep; the room was in almost as much chaos as yesterday. She began to quietly clear up the mess.

'Shanna.'

She turned with a start to find Rick looking at her, his eyes still fevered and bloodshot. 'I—I thought you were asleep.' She ran one of her hands nervously down her skirt-covered thigh.

He shook his head, wincing as the movement obviously hurt him. 'I was just resting,' his voice was still pure gravel. 'I didn't hear you come in.'

'You left the door open again.'

'It's easier for people to get in that way,' he shrugged.

'I agree,' she said dryly. 'Including thieves. Only a

wealthy man would be staying in a suite like this, and
that open door is an invitation someone isn't going to
refuse.'

'I know—you. Come to give me another blanket
bath, Shanna?' he teased.

He obviously felt slightly better than yesterday; he
hadn't even been up to his mocking humour then. But
she could see he was still far from well. 'That
depends.' She checked the bedclothes; they were
damp again. 'Has this jug been refilled since last
night?' It stood empty on his bedside cabinet again.

'No. Depends on what, Shanna?' he prompted softly.

'Things. Why didn't you call down for more juice?'
she demanded sternly. 'The telephone is just here.
Rest and lots of fluids, the doctor told you.'

'You've been talking to Cindy,' he grimaced. 'And
this is a hotel, not a hospital.'

'Exactly,' she said with satisfaction, opening his
wardrobe to pull out a suitcase and beginning to pack
some of his shirts into it.

'What are you doing?' he frowned as she took
underwear out of the dressing-table drawers and put
them in the suitcase too.

She turned to face him. 'This *is* a hotel, not the
place for someone who feels ill. There's no one to care
for you here. You're coming home with me.' She
looked at him with challenge.

'And you'll take care of me?'

'Yes!'

'Sounds good,' he said softly. 'Although you'll have
to help me get dressed.'

'Help is what you're going to get a lot of the next
couple of days,' she told him, just relieved he wasn't
arguing with her; she had expected him to!

'I take it you have a spare bedroom?' he drawled as
she helped him into his clothes.

Shanna smiled. 'You'll soon be back to normal! And yes, I have a spare room. You don't think I want your germs, do you?'

'No,' he sighed. 'You've made it clear you don't want anything I have to give.'

She gave him a sharp look at how bitterly he spoke the words, but he was looking too ill by this time for her to pursue the argument.

It wasn't easy getting him down to her car, but somehow she managed it, leaving him there to go back up and collect his things, leaving instructions for the room to be cleaned. He certainly didn't want to come back to that mess!

Her apartment was almost as impersonal as the hotel suite they had just left, but at least she could make Rick more comfortable there, would only be in the next bedroom at night if he should need anything. She felt better just knowing he was there; she hoped he felt the same way.

'I'll have to go back to the office for a few hours,' she told him after she had organised his lunch of a little hot soup and dry bread, having comfortably settled him in the single bed in her spare room. 'After all, I have to earn the money you pay me,' she added teasingly.

'If you weren't leaving I'd give you a raise. Maybe I'll give you a bonus anyway,' Rick added thoughtfully. 'No one has ever done anything like this for me before.'

'Maybe you just didn't give them the chance to.' Her tone was brittle in her embarrassment. 'You aren't the easiest of men to be kind to, Rick.'

'Now don't spoil it!' his mouth quirked.

'I won't,' she grinned. 'And the only bonus I need is for you to get well again and go back to your hotel.'

'I suppose I deserved that,' he sighed. 'I'll be fine now, if you want to go.'

'In other words, get back to work,' she derided.

'I wish I felt well enough to offer you an alternative, but unfortunately, I don't,' he said with genuine regret.

For the first time she realised what a problem he was going to be once he started to feel better. Oh well, she mentally shrugged, she would handle that when the time came. 'You're sure you have everything?' she hesitated at the bedroom door. 'Nothing else I can get you before I leave?'

'Nothing, thanks. You're a very thoughtful nurse,' he smiled, suddenly looking boyish. 'I didn't wait for ever, did I, Shanna?'

'Sorry?' she frowned her puzzlement, wondering if he were delirious and perhaps she shouldn't go and leave him on his own after all.

'How many days ago was it you told me I would wait for ever to be invited to stay at your home?' he mocked.

Her mouth set at the taunt. 'I could always change my mind and get you a taxi back to your hotel,' she warned.

'You could,' he nodded. 'But you won't.' He lay back with a sigh of contentment after this confident statement, his eyes closed. One lid was raised as he sensed her presence still in the room. 'Changed your mind about leaving?'

'No,' she snapped. 'I'm just wondering if you aren't already back on the way to recovery.'

'Do I look it?' he derided.

No, he didn't, he still looked ill. 'I'll get your dinner as soon as I get home,' she didn't answer him. 'Try and get some sleep while I'm gone.'

'I'm trying.'

'Ungrateful swine!' she muttered on her way out.

She sought out Cindy when she got back to the

office, and found the other woman in the canteen
having her afternoon break.

'A shot of caffeine to keep me going until the end of
the day.' She sipped her black coffee.

Shanna sat down opposite her, but got no drink for
herself, having wasted enough of the day already. 'I
just wanted to let you know that Rick is with me, in
case you go to his suite and get worried because he
isn't there.'

'Rick—is—with—you?' Cindy repeated disbelievingly. 'You mean at your home?'

Shanna swallowed hard, knowing how damning this
must seem after yesterday. 'I couldn't just leave him in
the hotel,' she tried to explain. 'It was so impersonal,
and he looked so awful. I went to the hotel this
morning and took him back to my apartment.'

'So that's where you were.' Cindy's frown cleared.
'Gloria was very evasive as to where you'd gone when
I asked her.'

'That's because she didn't know.' Shanna's smile
was tight. 'It isn't something I want broadcast,' she
gave Cindy an expressive look. ' 'Flu doesn't usually
last very long, another couple of days and Rick will be
well enough to come back to the hotel. I'd rather no
rumours started—erroneous rumours, of us co-
habiting.' She was aware of how pompous she
sounded, but she couldn't impress on Cindy enough
how innocent Rick being at her apartment was.

'You can rely on me,' Cindy grinned. 'I may put my
foot in my mouth every time I open it, but I certainly
know when to keep it closed. Although the others are
going to be curious as to where the boss has gone, and
some of them couldn't keep a secret if their life
depended on it,' she grimaced.

Shanna sighed, realising the embarrassing position
her 'good deed for the day' had put her in. 'What was

I supposed to do,' she said moodily, 'leave him there alone to suffer?'

Cindy held up her hands defensively. 'Hey, I haven't said a word!'

'But everyone else is going to!' groaned Shanna. 'There's no way I can keep something like this to myself, is there?'

'Well . . .'

'Always supposing Rick wants to keep it quiet,' she frowned. 'I wouldn't put it past him to have all his calls transferred to my apartment,' she grimaced. 'I should have just left him there to suffer in his own sweat,' she muttered.

Cindy shook her head. 'You don't have it in you to be that unfeeling. When I first heard that Rick was getting the run-around from a frosty lady called Shanna Logan I thought you must be a snobby bitch who thought herself too good for him.'

'And?' Shanna taunted, interested in spite of herself.

'No snobby bitch, just a lady who's been hurt in the past and doesn't intend to be again. Rick doesn't have a very good record in long-lasting relationships,' Cindy shrugged.

Shanna's laugh was completely lacking in humour. 'Whatever gave you the impression I've been hurt?'

'I'm an expert on relationships that go wrong,' Cindy said ruefully. 'I recognise the signs.'

Shanna shook her head. 'You're wrong this time,' her voice was sharp. 'My marriage was just about as perfect as I could have wished for.'

The other girl gave her a searching look, seeming to give a mental shrug. 'I have to get back to work,' she stood up. 'Rick may be ill, but he'll still expect all the work to be done when he gets back on his feet. Give him my love, won't you?' She raised a hand in parting, her head back as she walked past Jack making his way to their table.

Now Shanna understood the other woman's abrupt departure; nowadays Cindy avoided Jack wherever possible.

Jack sat down opposite her, giving her his usual leering smile. 'Cindy got herself a new boy-friend?' he drawled.

Shanna frowned, not liking this man at all, finding him too familiar for her tastes. 'Sorry?' she blinked.

'I overheard her tell you to give her love to someone,' he shrugged. 'I assumed it was a new boy-friend.'

'Not at all.' She got to her feet, deciding she might as well tell the 'town-crier' as have smutty rumours running through the building. The last thing she wanted was snide sniggers behind her and Rick's backs. 'She was asking me to give Rick her love when I see him—he's staying at my apartment at the moment,' she announced tautly. 'Any message *you* would like me to give him?'

Jack looked taken aback by her blasé attitude, although he recovered well. 'Not that I can think of, although you might tell him he's a lucky devil,' he added suggestively.

She nodded coolly. 'I'll tell him.'

'No! I mean—I was only joking, Shanna.' He looked less than confident that either she or Rick would appreciate his humour.

'I understand that, Mr Priest,' she said with sweet insincerity. 'Let's hope Rick sees it the same way, hmm?' she taunted.

'There's no need to tell him,' Jack blustered. 'I didn't mean anything by it,' he muttered.

'I'm sure you didn't,' she continued in the same saccharine voice. 'As I'm sure you'll correct anyone

else who gains the impression that Rick is staying with
me for any other reason than his illness?'

He gave her a speculative look, but agreed readily
enough. She had the feeling that there was one man
who was still unconvinced as to the innocence of
Rick's stay with her, but that he would slam into
anyone else who dared to suggest it was more than
that. Jack Priest might be a womaniser and a flirt, but
he knew that it wouldn't be wise to antagonise a boss
like Rick Dalmont, especially when he had no idea of
just how deep her involvement with Rick was. For the
moment she had an ally, albeit a reluctant one.

Rick was asleep when she looked quietly into his
room later that evening. He had been asleep since her
arrival home an hour earlier, and she had been careful
not to wake him, knowing that the sleep would help
him as much, if not more, than any dinner she could
give him.

She ate her dinner alone, her usual salad and cold
meat, tidying away neatly afterwards. The apartment
was as cold and stark as usual, although tonight there
was a difference. She was very conscious of Rick in the
spare bedroom.

She switched the television on softly, beginning to
doze in the chair, once again feeling the tiredness that
seemed to be increasing of late.

'Shanna?'

She was instantly awake, turning to find Rick
standing in the bedroom doorway, swaying slightly
on his feet, although he had had the forethought to
pull on his robe first! 'You shouldn't be out of
bed,' she stood up, pushing down her own feelings
of weakness.

He leant against the doorframe, very pale, a gaunt
look to his face. 'I called out to you,' he told her
gruffly. 'You didn't hear me. You were so white just

now, Shanna. I thought you—Do you always sleep so deeply?' he frowned.

'Yes.' Her answer was abrupt as she reached his side. 'Now go back to bed.'

'I need to go to the bathroom.'

She helped him through to the other room, sitting down in a chair to wait for him, feeling too tired to stand any longer. Thank goodness it was the weekend tomorrow and she could have a lie-in, although with Rick about the place it didn't look like being a restful time.

She prepared him a late dinner once he was back in his room, watching over him as he managed to eat a little of the omelette, making sure he drank the fresh orange-juice she had given him with it.

'I'm going to bed now,' she told him a little after nine.

'Bed?' he blinked, his jaw clean-shaven, having shaved and washed while he was in the bathroom, applying a tangy aftershave to his jaw too. 'But it's early.'

'And I'm tired,' she said flatly.

'No party tonight?'

'Not while I have a guest, no,' she answered stiffly.

He looked at her with dark mocking eyes. 'Guests are usually—entertained.'

He was recovering fast, she could tell that, his humour and outspoken comments coming more frequently this evening. 'You want entertainment?' her eyes gleamed vengefully.

His brows rose. 'Yes.'

'Right.' She left the room, coming back a few minutes later. 'Your entertainment,' she said triumphantly.

Rick looked blankly at the portable television set she had placed on the dressing-table, then he turned angry black eyes on her. 'What the hell do you mean by bringing that in here——'

'You wanted entertainment,' she shrugged. 'There it is.' She grinned at him. 'Isn't television what you had in mind, Rick?'

He scowled. 'If I thought I could catch you I'd get out of this bed and give you the beating you deserve. How dare you carry that heavy thing in here? You could have injured yourself!'

It was slowly dawning on her that his anger was directed at the fact that she had carried the television in here, not because he had been given that as his entertainment. 'It's portable——'

'What does that mean?' he dismissed scathingly. 'Just that it has a handle on the top of it to transport it by! It doesn't make it weigh any less.'

'Rick——'

'Don't ever do anything like that again!' he was glaring at her now. 'Not even to get in a low-blow at me.'

She flushed at the rebuke. 'Do you want the television on or not? I'm going to bed.'

'Not,' he snapped. 'Television happens to be my least favourite form of entertainment.'

'I can guess what tops the list!'

'I doubt it,' he drawled. 'Women are a necessary part of my life, Shanna, as I've already admitted, but they aren't a really enjoyable part. They demand too much and give too little in return.'

'Then what do you enjoy?' she asked, interested in spite of herself.

He lay back against the pillows. 'I have a ranch in Montana, in the mountains, right alongside my parents' place. Some day I'm going to retire there like my dad did.'

She could see how the thought pleased him. 'Why

not now?' she frowned. 'Surely you're wealthy enough not to keep on with this merry-go-round?'

'Yes,' he said without conceit. 'And I can't deny I like being there, but at the moment there's nothing to hold me. I have someone to run the ranch for me, and the house is too big for one man. Maybe when I have a wife and children . . .' he shrugged.

Her eyes widened. 'You intend marrying?' He had never given that impression.

'One day,' he nodded.

'And having children?'

'They usually come along with the wife,' he smiled ruefully.

'Yes,' she said flatly. 'Well, if you need anything, just call me,' she added briskly.

'Would you hear me?' he derided her heavy sleeping.

She grimaced. 'Probably not.'

'That's what I thought. Okay, Shanna I'll see you in the morning. I like coffee with my breakfast, by the way.'

'Because it wakes you up,' she drawled.

'You remembered,' he grinned.

'I remember a lot of things about you, Rick Dalmont,' she warned. 'And most of them are bad.'

His husky laugh followed her from the room, although her own smile faded as soon as she closed her bedroom door; the talk of wives and families was upsetting her.

She awoke to the sound of china rattling against china, opening her eyes to find Rick standing next to her bed, fully dressed today in faded close-fitting denims and a black silk shirt, a tray of tea and biscuits in his hand.

Shanna sat up with a start, pushing the dark hair from her face, feeling strangely vulnerable without her make-up, the sheet pulled up to her chin as she looked at him questioningly.

'It's after ten,' he explained gently, putting the tray down. 'I was awake at seven.' He sat on the side of the bed, frowning his concern. 'I'm beginning to wonder who should be looking after who.'

She sipped her tea. 'You're obviously feeling better,' she said briskly.

'A little,' he conceded. 'Although my small burst of energy seems to have tired me. But at least I felt refreshed when I woke up, you look more tired today than you did last night.'

'That often happens,' she dismissed. 'It's just the tiredness catching up with me. I'll be fine once I've showered and eaten breakfast.'

'I'm not so sure——'

'No one asked you to be,' she told him waspishly. 'Now get out of my bedroom—I don't remember telling you you could just walk in here any time you felt like it.'

He raised mocking brows. 'Does that mean you don't want the tea?' he taunted.

'Get out of here,' she sighed wearily.

To her surprise he went without further argument, the apartment in silence now, so she assumed he had gone back to his own room. The tea and biscuits were very welcome, although she had no intention of telling Rick that; she didn't want him to make a habit of coming into her bedroom. What was she thinking of— of course he wouldn't make a habit of it, he was leaving as soon as he was feeling better!

He was back in bed by the time she was up and dressed, asleep by the look of him, and from the mess he had left in the kitchen he had prepared himself some eggs for breakfast.

She took no risk of him causing that much havoc

again in her kitchen by preparing a late dinner for him when he woke up, the two of them eating it in the kitchen.

'I hope you don't mind,' Rick looked across the table at her as they lingered over the strong coffee he had made for them. 'I used your telephone to call Cindy this morning.'

'Feel free,' she invited lightly.

'She said you'd already explained.'

'I did,' she nodded. 'I also told your P.R. man to watch what he thinks, let alone what he says!'

Rick smiled. 'I imagine Jack has been suitably put in his place.'

'Very suitably,' she confirmed tightly.

'Just what did you tell Cindy?' he mused.

She shrugged. 'The truth.'

'You do a lot for my ego,' he grimaced.

'I didn't realise you would want people to believe you were here for any other reason than the real one?'

'I guess not,' he shrugged. 'It was a good meal, Shanna,' he complimented.

'Thank you.' Shanna stood up to clear away. 'Shouldn't you go back to bed now?'

'Another invitation, Shanna?'

She turned to find him standing very close to her, closer than she had realised, and she recoiled back as she almost touched him. 'Would you please go back to bed?' she said tautly. 'I just have to tidy up here and then I'm going to bed myself.'

Rick looked down at her for long timeless minutes, half a dozen different emotions flickering in his eyes, all of them too fleeting to be analysed. Finally he nodded. 'I'll see you in the morning.'

'Er—Rick,' she stopped him at the door, 'I think you should leave tomorrow,' she told him as he slowly turned.

He seemed about to argue, then he shrugged. 'All right. Late tomorrow. I suppose it must have been forty-eight-hour 'flu, huh?'

'I suppose,' she agreed softly, just wishing he would go, leave her alone.

He nodded. 'Tomorrow.'

'Yes,' and she turned away.

She knew he had gone, could sense it, her fingers clutching on to the work unit in front of her. It was a strange feeling having Rick here, knowing there was someone else in her home. It wasn't an unpleasant feeling, just a forgotten one. Rick's manner today was definitely that of a predatory male as he regained his strength. She had become used to her privacy; she wasn't sure she liked having to check the bathroom was free before she went in there, having to be careful she was always fully dressed. Just having Rick here at all made her feel uncomfortable.

It was even worse the next day. The tension built up inside her as the day progressed, just longing for the time Rick said he was leaving. He seemed in no hurry to do so.

He prowled around the lounge after dinner, stopping to pick up a photograph of Perry that stood on the side table. 'Good likeness,' he muttered.

'Very good.' Shanna moved to take the photograph out of his hand.

'I've noticed a lot of them about the apartment,' he persisted in spite of her pale face.

'Why not?' she said sharply. 'Perry was my husband.'

'Was,' Rick agreed grimly. 'But he's dead.'

She drew in a ragged breath. 'Isn't it time you left? It's getting late.'

His mouth tightened, his hands now thrust into the pockets of his denims, the blue shirt stretched tautly across his chest. 'You can't wait for me to leave, can you?' he bit out angrily. 'Well, okay, I'll go! I'll get my things and be out of your hair in a couple of minutes. Will that satisfy you?'

She didn't answer him, but stood still clutching on to the photograph of Perry, holding it protectively in front of her. The bedroom door slammed behind Rick and she could hear him moving about the room as he threw his things in his suitcase.

The tears flowed down her cheeks, as she looked down at Perry's photograph. He had been so young, so full of life, and now he was dead, dead, *dead* . . .

She stiffened as the bedroom door opened, knowing that Rick was leaving, that after today he might never be back. And she suddenly knew the reason for her tension all day, knew that she didn't want him to go.

'I'm going now,' he said softly, the anger having left his voice at least. 'Thanks for taking care of me. I— Shanna?' he frowned as she turned, the tears still wet on her cheeks.

'I——' her voice came out as a shaky croak, and she swallowed convulsively. 'Rick, don't—don't go.' She licked the tears from her lips, looking at him pleadingly. 'Please don't go!'

'Hey, of course not, if you don't want me to.' He pulled her into his arms, holding her gently.

She clung to him unashamedly, needing his warmth, his strength. 'I'm so frightened at times,' she quivered against him. 'So frightened of being alone,' she admitted the accusation he had once levelled at her.

'We all are, honey,' he murmured into her silky hair.

'Even you?' she trembled.

'Even me,' he nodded. 'Now do you want to watch television, or let me beat you at Monopoly again?' he teased her with the fact that he had beaten her at the game twice this afternoon. 'You just name it and we'll do it,' he told her indulgently.

She looked up at him with unwavering green eyes. 'Make love to me, Rick.'

His breath seemed to catch in his throat, looking at her as if he couldn't quite believe what he had just heard. 'Shanna——'

'I need you, Rick,' she admitted softly. 'I need to feel wanted, loved. Would you please make love to me?'

He drew in a ragged breath. 'You're sure this is what you want? You aren't going to hate me—afterwards?'

She could never hate this man, she knew that now, knew that the thought of him leaving tonight filled her with despair, that she had come to rely on him, to need him, that she had done the one thing she had sworn would never happen again—she had fallen in love, and with Rick Dalmont.

'No,' she moved easily back into his arms, giving herself to him in that moment. 'I won't ever hate you.'

CHAPTER NINE

AFTERWARDS she lay cradled in his arms, the tears of ecstasy she had cried as he possessed her dry on her cheeks now, the even tenor of Rick's breathing beneath her telling her that he had already fallen asleep.

It had been beautiful between them; Rick had taken her with a mixture of tenderness and passion that had her crying out his name as wave after wave of pleasure flowed between them as if it would never stop.

And when it had stopped the closeness had still been there, Rick telling her over and over again how beautiful she was.

Her arms tightened about him now, this man she had discovered she loved. She had no delusions that she meant any more to him than the dozens of other women he had made love to and forgotten, but she was glad she had known him, that they had become lovers. And when the time came for her to be forgotten by him she would let him go without reproach. He would never know of her love for him, never know of the happiness he had given her when she had thought only loneliness remained.

Finally she drifted off to sleep herself, although she was conscious of Rick's possessive hold on her all night, as if he thought she might leave him if he didn't hold her tightly.

He was already awake when the alarm clock went off at seven, reaching over her to switch it off, bending over her sleep-drugged face as she opened her eyes. 'Good morning,' he greeted throatily, almost uncertainly.

She knew the reason for the emotion, knew he doubted her reaction to their lovemaking of last night. She smiled up at him sleepily. 'Good morning, Rick. You're very nice to wake up to,' she told him huskily.

'I am?' Still he hesitated.

'Do you doubt it?'

'I doubt a lot of things where you're concerned,' he admitted with a self-derisive smile. 'For a moment when I woke up this morning I thought I'd dreamt the whole thing, that I was still delirious from the 'flu and had imagined you. Then I felt you curved against me and I knew it was all true. Shanna, I wouldn't have stayed last night if you hadn't wanted me to. Oh, I wanted to stay, but I was through forcing myself on you.'

'And now?'

'Now I want to make love to you again,' he admitted softly.

She smiled up at him. 'I thought you'd never ask!'

He bent his head, his mouth moving against hers questioningly, as if he were still wary of the change in her. 'Shanna, what changed your mind?' He looked down at her with coal-black eyes.

'Didn't you know, it's a woman's prerogative?' she teased. 'And what changed yours? After we had dinner with Janice and Henry last week I thought you'd decided to give up on me. You didn't show the same reluctance last night.'

'I "gave up on you", as you put it, because you'd made it plain that you would do anything to thwart me, even down to denying you had had an idea similar to mine. It seemed obvious that you really disliked me, that I could go on chasing after you for ever and not get anywhere. I'm not a masochist, Shanna, I'll only hit my head against a wall for so long, then I decide the pain isn't worth it.'

'I'm really sorry about the problem page—I was being childish.' She shook her head. 'You bring out the worst in me, for some reason, and I oppose you even when I don't really want to. I've liked all the new ideas you've brought into the magazine, including Cindy as the new editor. She's going to accept, by the way.'

'Good,' he nodded his satisfaction. 'I'm sure she'll make a good job of it.'

'So am I.'

Rick's eyes darkened. 'You could still change your mind——'

'I don't want to.' The last thing she wanted was to be anywhere near Rick in six months' or a year's time. No, an affair now, an affair that ended when he became bored with her, was much more agreeable to her. She wanted to be well away from Rick when the weakness became a final blackness.

'Sure?' His gaze probed.

'Very,' she smiled up at him, dispelling the impression of vulnerability she had acquired the last few minutes. 'Now do you usually have lengthy conversations with your women at this time of the morning?' she mocked.

'No,' he laughed throatily. 'Most of my "women" are still asleep at this time of the morning.'

'Ah, but they don't have jobs to go to.'

His hand gently caressed her pale cheek. 'We could take the day off, Shanna. Do something crazy like go for a boat-trip in the park.'

'In the winter?' she teased.

'Well, I said it was crazy!'

'It's also impossible—you can't get boats out in the winter. There isn't the trade, you know,' she added mockingly. 'Besides, Mr Dalmont, haven't you taken enough time off lately without playing truant for the day?'

'Slave-driver!'

'Someone has to keep you in line.' She threw back the bedclothes. 'Now as we seem to have wasted all this time talking, would you like to use the bathroom first or shall I?'

Rick pinned her back to the bed, his hands on her shoulders, one of his legs thrown casually across hers. 'I want *you* before I do anything else.'

'So you're a morning man,' she derided.

'And an afternoon one. And an evening one too,' he grinned.

'In other words, you're insatiable?' Her arms curved about his neck.

'At the moment, yes.'

None of last night had been a dream for either of them, if anything their lovemaking was more explosive than ever.

It was after eight when they finally got out of bed, only time left for them both to have a quick shower and drive to work.

Rick held out his hands for her car keys. 'I was in a state of delirium when I let you drive me from the hotel,' he mocked as he got in behind the wheel.

Shanna sat next to him in the passenger seat. 'And when I drove you back from Henry's?' she taunted.

His expression became bland as he shrugged. 'You aren't a bad driver, Shanna. And you don't cook well enough to be planning the day's menus as you go along.'

'Just for that you can cook dinner tonight!'

He gave her a searching look. 'I'm invited?'

'Yes.'

'I can stay tonight?'

'Yes.'

His throat moved convulsively. 'Can I move in with you?'

'If you'd like to,' she nodded.

'I'd like to,' he confirmed huskily.

'And I'd like you to too,' she said briskly. 'So that's settled.'

'Shanna——'

'No questions, no post-mortems,' she pleaded. 'Let's just enjoy what we have for the moment.'

'Is that what you really want?' His eyes were narrowed.

'Yes,' she answered abruptly, knowing it was the only answer she could give.

'Okay,' he sighed.

If she didn't know better she would have said it wasn't what Rick wanted at all. But she did know better, and she was determined to show him that she wanted no more from him than any of his other women had expected, that the affair was as casual to her as it was to him.

The atmosphere in their shared office was so much lighter today, and she knew that everyone who came in to see one or both of them was aware of the subtle difference in their relationship. At first she felt some discomfort, never having been in this position before, not used to being thought of as any man's mistress. But the open seduction in Rick's eyes whenever he looked at her more than made up for it; the smiles they shared were warm and intimate.

'God, what a day!' he groaned into her hair when they reached his suite to pick up some more of his things.

'I quite enjoyed it.' She sounded puzzled.

'It was too damned long,' he growled against her throat. 'And I'm sure that half the people who came in to see us today only did it out of curiosity.'

Shanna laughed softly as he scowled. 'I didn't mind.'

'I did,' he muttered. 'Every time I decided I just had to kiss you someone came in.'

'We're alone now,' she encouraged, feeling the excitement of being in his arms, the moist warmth of his lips against her throat.

He didn't need any further encouragement, removing her clothes with infinite enjoyment, allowing her to do the same to him, then the huge double bed welcomed the weight of their bodies.

'Shanna darling . . .!' Rick cried as pleasure enveloped his body, shuddering with the delight of possessing her once again. 'I've been longing to do that all day,' he chuckled against her breast. 'You have a very sexy body, sweetheart, and seeing you walk about all day has been torture for my self-control.'

Shanna was totally exhausted, too weak even to speak, unable to stop the waves of sleep that swept over her, and Rick's voice reached her as if from a distance, a great distance.

It was dark when she woke up, and Rick was no longer beside her in the bed. It took her several minutes to wake up enough to get up and go in search of him, pulling on one of his shirts over her nakedness, her own clothes still scattered about the lounge where Rick had thrown them.

He sat in one of the comfortable armchairs drinking what looked like whisky, staring off into space, although there were some open papers on the table in front of him. Shanna moved to put her arms about him from behind, kissing him on the mouth as he turned his head sideways, tasting the whisky on his lips.

'Mm,' he groaned his satisfaction a few seconds later. 'And how is my Sleeping Beauty?' He pulled her round so that she sat across his knees, her arms still about his neck.

'Awake,' she murmured against his chin, nibbling lightly.

'Just,' he nodded as she stifled a yawn. 'Why don't you get dressed and we'll have dinner sent up? We may as well stay here tonight, it's already late.'

'How late?' she frowned.

'After nine. By the time we've eaten——'

'We can eat at the flat,' she insisted.

'Not if I'm cooking,' Rick shook his head. 'Let's eat here, sweetheart. I'm sure neither of us is in the mood to cook tonight.'

Shanna wasn't even sure she was in the mood to eat, let alone cook, but she didn't want to spend the night in his hotel room. She struggled to sit up, but his arms remained firm about her. 'Rick, please let me go. I want to shower and dress.'

'You still look tired.' He touched the dark shadows beneath her eyes.

She forced a tight smile to her lips. 'Can I help it if you're a demanding lover?'

'Can I help it if you're so damned beautiful I can't keep my hands off you?' he smiled.

'And can I help it if I can't resist you?' she joined in the teasing.

'You managed to do just that until yesterday,' he grimaced.

'When I couldn't resist the Dalmont charm any longer,' she taunted.

'I should have got 'flu earlier,' he grinned. 'I never realised you had the nursing instinct in you.'

'Well, now you know,' she mocked, swinging away from him. 'Rick, I don't want to stay here. I don't want to be just another Anna Kalder.'

'Anna?' he frowned. 'You know about her?'

'I know she was your mistress for a few weeks. But then so have a lot of women been.' She couldn't keep the bitterness out of her voice, try as she might. 'I won't be kept at your hotel like all those other women. If you care anything for me at all please let's go to my apartment.'

'Shanna——'

'*Please*, Rick,' she looked at him with pleading eyes.

'Okay, okay,' he sighed. 'But could we just eat first—I'm starved! We could eat in the restaurant downstairs if you would prefer it.'

'That won't be necessary—up here will be fine. But I want to leave straight afterwards.' She went back to the bedroom and into the shower, feeling refreshed under the cool spray, regretting her argument with Rick but still determined she wouldn't become just another of his women, moving in here with him until he threw her out. When it came time for someone to leave it wasn't going to be her!

She was dressed when Rick came into the bedroom, unable to meet his gaze as she retouched her make-up.

'Honey, I'm sorry.' His arms came about her from behind, pulling her back against him. 'But surely you know you're different, special? And no, I don't tell all my women that,' he said dryly. 'You really are special. And if I've upset you I'm sorry. I didn't realise you felt this way about staying here. We'll go back to your apartment now.'

'What about dinner?' She looked at him with wide eyes.

'We'll eat when we get to the apartment—if we feel hungry.' The look in his eyes told her food wasn't what he had on his mind for when they reached her home.

It had been strange having Rick about the apartment during his illness, but it was even stranger looking across the room at him and knowing by the look in his eyes that soon they would be in bed together, their bodies entwined as they made love.

The knowledge that she could arouse Rick that easily gave her a glow of satisfaction, and she knew that not even on her honeymoon with Perry had she spent so much time in a man's arms, feeling cherished and needed. Rick held nothing back, completely honest in his desire for her, and as the days passed, as three weeks passed, she began to wonder when he was going to tire of her. His affairs never lasted long—he wasn't usually in one place long enough to maintain them!—and yet he gave no indication of wanting to leave her. It was then that Shanna really began to worry, to know that she might have to be the one who ended their relationship. She had envisaged a brief affair with Rick, and hadn't wanted any more than that.

He brought her breakfast in bed on their fourth Saturday together, sitting in the chair and watching her indulgently as she ate the scrambled eggs and toast he had prepared for her. 'I could quite get used to this.' He sat back with a lazy stretch of satisfaction.

Shanna looked up from drinking her coffee, hoping the love she felt for this man didn't glow in her eyes, but very much afraid that it did. 'To what?' she asked softly.

There had been a lot of gentleness and pleasure between them the last three weeks, and even working together in the day hadn't diminished Rick's consideration for her. Everyone at the magazine was aware of their changed status now, and the curiosity about them faded somewhat as their relationship continued to flourish.

'Domesticity,' he smiled. 'It feels good to wake up in the morning and feel you beside me. I even enjoy spoiling you with breakfast in bed occasionally. And I more than enjoy our nights together,' he teased.

So did she. It seemed as if Rick only had to touch her for her to be trembling with desire, and not a night had passed without that desire flaming between them at least once. Sometimes their lovemaking would take them through until dawn, when they would finally sleep satiated in each other's arms. It was at these times that her body felt so drained of strength she felt as if she might never wake up, and although Rick occasionally mentioned her tiredness he didn't pursue the subject.

'How about you?' he prompted softly.

She shrugged. 'I've enjoyed our time together too. But it can't last, can it?' Her tone was light, her eyes unblinking as she saw his face darken with displeasure.

'Why can't it?' he demanded.

She sat back against the pillows with a sigh. 'How long do your affairs usually last?'

'This is diff——'

'How long, Rick? What was the longest relationship you ever had?'

'Shanna——'

'Please, Rick, this is important!'

His mouth tightened. 'I think—six weeks,' he muttered.

'And we've already been together three and a half weeks,' she pointed out.

'That has noth—Damn!' he rasped as the ringing of the telephone interrupted him. 'I'll get it,' he told her as she went to get out of bed, her nakedness in front of him something she no longer felt embarrassed about.

She let him go; most of the calls to her flat lately had been for him anyway. She could hear him talking on the telephone for several seconds, and then he came back to the bedroom.

'It's for you,' he told her flatly. 'Henry,' he murmured as she reached the door.

Shanna hesitated only fractionally, before pulling on her robe to go and talk to her brother. She had seen nothing of Henry the last few weeks, although she had spoken to him several times on the telephone. As far as she was aware, he knew nothing of Rick staying here. Although that might not be true now!

'Hello, Henry,' she greeted calmly.

'Shanna? Is everything all right? Rick said you were in bed.' Her brother's concern could be clearly heard.

'I was,' she said dryly. 'He'd just given me my breakfast.'

There was silence at the other end of the line for several long seconds. 'He's there rather early, isn't he?' Henry sounded confused.

'Not really, he was here rather late.'

'Shanna . . .? Is it true, then, is he living with you?' her brother demanded. 'There's been talk, but I couldn't believe it.'

'Believe it,' she said dully. 'Rick's been staying here for almost a month.'

'Shanna!' Henry sounded deeply shocked.

She sighed. 'You were the one who thought I should go out with him,' she reminded him.

'But I didn't mean you to set up house with him!'

'I haven't set up house with him,' she snapped. 'I'm not living with him either. Both those terms imply a sort of permanence to the relationship, and we all know there's nothing permanent about this.'

Henry gave a deep sigh. 'You're twenty-five years old, old enough to know your own mind, but I can't help but be surprised about this affair with Rick.'

'I know,' she sympathised gently. 'And I'm sorry.'

'Don't apologise, Shanna, it's really none of my business. Actually, I telephoned to ask you over for dinner one evening—we haven't seen you for weeks. You'd better bring Rick with you, I suppose,' he added grudgingly.

'I'll sort out an evening and get back to you,' she promised. 'Give my love to Janice and the children.'

'Shanna!' he stopped her ringing off.

'Yes?' she was wary now.

'Take care, won't you?'

Her mouth twisted. 'Yes, Henry, I'll take care. And I'll call you soon.' She turned from ringing off to find Rick scowling across the room at her.

'What did he mean by that last remark?' he rasped. 'Does he think I'm irresponsible enough to get you pregnant?'

'Rick——'

'Because I wouldn't do that to you.'

'I know that,' she soothed him, going over to lightly touch his arm. 'Rick, he's my brother, he's naturally concerned for me. I'm sure he didn't mean anything by what he said just now.'

'I should damn well hope not!' His arms came about her. 'How would it look if you were pregnant when I introduce you to my parents?'

Shanna stiffened, pulling back to look up at him. 'Your parents?' she repeated softly.

He grimaced. 'Sweetheart, I didn't want to tell you like this, but it doesn't look as if I have any choice. There've been some problems in the States that I have to go back and sort out. I thought you could come with me, meet my parents at the same time.'

'No!' She moved out of his arms, standing some distance away from him. 'I have no intention of going to America as your mistress.'

His expression darkened. 'Who said anything about a mistress?' His eyes were narrowed to black slits. 'I may be thirty-seven years old, but my father would bodily throw me out of the house if I introduced one of my mistresses to my mother. I want to take you to them as my wife, Shanna. I was trying to ask you to marry me when Henry called just now.'

Marriage. It wasn't a word she associated with Rick, it wasn't something she had even thought of in connection with him, and she couldn't think of it now either.

'Shanna?' He sounded anxious as she didn't answer him. 'Honey, this wasn't the way I had it planned, just blurting it out like this, but I love you, and I want to marry you. I don't like the impression your brother has of our relationship, I don't like anyone thinking that about you, but at the time it was all you would accept. Honey, please answer me, will you marry me?'

Shanna swallowed hard at the ragged pain in his voice, wishing with all her heart and soul that she could throw herself into his arms and never have to leave. 'I—I can't,' she turned away. 'I can't, Rick!'

Pain flickered across his face, his eyes were darker than ever. 'I know something about your first marriage has made you wary of that sort of commitment, but whatever it was, it doesn't apply to us. God, I'm not even asking that you love me in return, all I want is for you to let me love *you*, take care of you.'

She chewed on her bottom lip to stop it trembling, overwhelmed by the wealth of love Rick was showing her. She hadn't believed he was capable of loving like this, and yet she couldn't doubt him, could see it all in his face, in his eyes. And she loved him *so much* in return.

'Cindy once told me,' she moistened her lips nervously, 'she told me you don't bet on losers. I'm a loser, Rick. I'd be no good for you.'

'I'm sure Cindy wasn't referring to you when she spoke about losers. And I happen to think you're very good for me. I want you for my wife, Shanna,' he repeated firmly.

'I can't!' she repeated raggedly.

'Why the hell not?' he rasped, not used to opposition in anything. 'You would never want for anything as my wife, and I can't continue living like this. I moved in here with you because you made it plain you wouldn't accept marriage then, but I have to leave next week, and I don't intend going without you.'

'You'll have to,' she said dully.

'No——'

'Yes!' she told him forcefully. 'Can't you understand, I don't *want* to marry you!'

His breathing was harsh and ragged as he looked at her as if he had never seen her before. 'What's that supposed to mean? You don't love me? What?'

'Work it out, Rick,' she sighed wearily, wishing he would just go away and stop torturing her.

'I'm okay for an affair, to go to bed with, but you don't want to marry me, is that it?' he bit out tautly. 'Answer me, damn you!' he moved to shake her roughly.

'Yes!' she cried. 'Yes, that's it exactly.' Her hair swung about her face where he shook her.

'*God!*' He pushed her away from him with an agonised groan; he was very pale, almost grey beneath his tan. 'I'll come back for my things later,' he spoke almost dazedly. 'I just have to get away from you.' He shook his head, pulling on his jacket, suddenly looking up at her with pained eyes. 'Why do I get the impression that this scene is exactly what you wanted?' he groaned. 'That you planned for me to walk out this way?'

Shanna paled at how astute he was. She had known of his intelligence, his quicksilver method of making decisions, but she hadn't realised he had come to know her this well, that he would guess exactly what she had been trying to do. She *did* want him to walk out; she knew it had to be his decision to walk away.

'Shanna, what are you hiding from me?' He was in command of himself again, had her pinned to the spot with his sharp gaze.

Nevertheless, she couldn't meet that gaze, and she looked anywhere but at him. 'You're imagining things,' she dismissed lightly. 'Why should I want to hide anything from you? We've had fun together, now it's over. Do you always take the end of an affair this seriously?' she mocked.

'An affair, no. But when the woman I love, the woman who has been my lover, who has seemed as if she cares for me a little in return, turns down a proposal of marriage in the cruel way you've done, then I know something is wrong. Why do you want me to hate you, Shanna?' he asked shrewdly. 'Why are you pushing me out of your life like this?'

'You're imagining things——'

'No!' his fist landed violently on the coffee table, although he didn't even flinch at the pain it must have caused. 'I'm not imagining a thing. Why is it imperative I get out of your life, and in a hurry?'

'Perhaps so that someone else can take your place!' she snapped.

He gave a tight smile. 'Careful, Shanna, your desperation is starting to show. I'm not going,' he told her hardly. 'Not until I have the truth from you. I know you're hiding something from—God!' he rushed forward to catch her as she swayed and fell. 'Shanna!' He looked down at her waxen features as he lay her down on the sofa, rubbing her numbed hands as consciousness faded and swam for several minutes.

As she watched the concern in his face turn to fear,

horror, she knew he had discovered her secret. It had always been a possibility, of course, one that she had tried to avoid him realising by trying to avoid *him*. But being with him these last weeks virtually twenty-four hours a day she had exposed her every weakness, and the truth now was in Rick's eyes.

'How long?' he croaked. 'How long have you known?'

She swallowed hard. 'Just over a year.'

'Perry knew?'

'Yes,' she confirmed with bitterness.

Rick was breathing heavily, swallowing convulsively, a nerve jumping erratically in his jaw. 'Can anything be done?'

'I don't know,' she said dully.

'God, you don't mean——'

'That I'm dying?' she finished flatly. 'I think so. Yes, I think I'm dying, Rick.' She touched the rigidness of his jaw as he seemed to flinch.

CHAPTER TEN

IT had come as much as a shock to her a year ago as it did to Rick now. Old people, people who had lived their lives, had had their children, their grandchildren, had heart complaints, not people of twenty-four! It had been just over a year ago when the doctor had told her of the defect, of the operations she had needed then to right the wrong. She had never had that operation, and the increasing weakness she felt lately seemed to say it might already be too late.

The possibility that Rick would realise had always been there, the shock of knowing his mother had a similar problem had told her that. He had grown up with the knowledge that his mother was ill, had known all her symptoms, although until this moment his desire for Shanna had blinded him to her own weakness being of a similar kind.

But he knew now; the full knowledge of it was in the pained blackness of his eyes. She hadn't meant for him to love her, had never dreamt that he would; she had believed she would just be another affair to him before he moved on. If she had even guessed his feelings for her could develop into something serious she would never have become involved with him. But it was too late for that now, too late for her to stop him loving her. She had caused him this pain, and there was nothing she could do about it.

'You *think* you are?' He shook her now, his expression intent. 'But you don't know for certain?'

She moistened her dry lips with the tip of her

tongue. 'Not for certain, no. But I've been feeling so weak lately, the tiredness has been more intense.'

Rick seemed to be thinking fast, each problem thought out quickly in his mind and dealt with. 'Do you have a doctor? Someone who's been dealing with your case?'

'Well, yes. But——'

'Who is he? What's his telephone number? Shanna!' he prompted hardly as she seemed dazed.

'I—He—It's in my bag,' she told him abruptly. 'But I haven't seen him for months.'

'Why the hell not?' he rasped, frantically throwing everything out of her bag on to the table, picking up a bottle of pills to frown at them for several seconds before once again searching through the papers he had taken out of her bag. 'Is this it?' He held up a card.

'Yes.' She swallowed hard, her expression turning to one of alarm as he began to dial the doctor's number. 'Rick, you can't call him now—it's a Saturday!'

He gave her a look that said he didn't care if it was three o'clock on a Sunday morning; he was calling the doctor. 'A damned recording,' he muttered a few seconds later, grabbing a pen off the table where it had been tipped out of her bag, scribbling down another number as it was obviously recited to him. 'Go and get dressed, Shanna,' he ordered as he re-dialled. 'I want to be able to leave as soon as possible after I've made this call. You—Sweetheart!' he groaned as she buried her face in her hands, crying uncontrollably. He slammed the receiver down to go to her, taking her in his arms, holding her tightly against him. 'I love you, Shanna. I love you,' he murmured the words over and over again until she stopped crying.

'I'm sorry,' she shuddered back to control. 'It's just that—You reacted so differently from Perry. He—

hated the thought of my being ill, of something inside me being wrong.'

Rick's arms tightened. 'Tell me about it, Shanna. Tell me what happened a year ago.'

She lay heavily against his chest, clinging to him but unable to look at him. 'We wanted children,' she wiped her cheek dry with the back of her hand. 'We'd been trying for some time, and so we—we both had medicals. Just general things, because Perry hated all things medical. He'd had so many accidents during the course of his career that he'd grown to hate the sight and smell of hospitals. The doctor found no reason why we couldn't have children, but he did find—he did find——' she stopped talking as her voice shook uncontrollably. 'He said I needed an operation, that if I didn't have it I would die——'

'Then why the hell didn't you have it?' Rick rasped.

'I couldn't have gone through it without Perry's support, and—well, as soon as he heard the result of the medicals he went out and crashed in a race. He injured his back and could no longer compete in races. He hated me to be anywhere near him, he began to resent me—blamed me for his accident. We had been so happy until then, but my health and his accident seemed to change everything. He—he—You know the rest!' she shuddered.

'Other women?'

'Yes,' she sighed. 'And drink. He was drunk when we had the accident that killed him. I wanted to drive, but he said he didn't want a—a cripple driving him, that I'd probably kill him. He was completely drunk when he drove into the brick wall. I don't know how it was kept out of the newspapers, and at the time I was past caring. Perry was dead, and they told me at the hospital then that my operation was imperative.'

'And?'

'And I just wanted to die!'

'You told me that two weeks after we met,' Rick frowned. 'But I couldn't believe you really meant it.'

'I meant it. I welcomed death, the idea of it. I loved Perry, and my illness repulsed him, made him hate me. I even went to work at *Fashion Lady* in the hope of showing him I could carry on a normal life, that nothing had changed.' She gave a bitter laugh. 'Even that backfired on me! After the first accident he had to give up his career, and the thought of his wife going out to work made him feel inadequate.'

'But you still loved him.'

'Yes!' she trembled.

'And now?'

'Now?' she blinked up at him.

'I've just told you I love you, Shanna,' he rasped. 'And if you think another man's inadequacies are going to rob me of *my* chance of a wife and children then you're mistaken!' His expression was harsh. 'Perry may have been the man you loved, but he was weak—*I'm* not. I want you to live, and you're *going* to.'

'But——'

'You're going to, Shanna,' he told her with conviction. 'One day I'm going to watch as you put *our* children to bed and kiss them goodnight. That was the night I realised I loved you, you know. I watched you laughing with Peter and Susan, watched your gentleness with them, and I knew that I wanted them to be our children, that I loved you. It was the biggest shock of my life,' he said self-derisively. 'Especially as you felt no reluctance to show me how little I meant to you.'

'I——'

'Yes?' he prompted sharply.

Shanna shook her head, biting her bottom lip. 'Nothing.'

He gave her a piercing look. 'You had me trapped, Shanna, and I didn't like the feeling,' he continued with a sigh. 'Hence Samantha, Carrie, Delia, and all the others,' he said grimly. 'All those beautiful women, and I didn't make love to any of them!'

'You didn't?' she gasped.

'No,' he admitted ruefully. 'I just felt more trapped than ever, just wanted to be with my woman with the jet-black hair and flashing green eyes. And although you said you didn't care for me it was you who looked after me when I had 'flu.'

'I would have done the same for anyone,' she blushed.

'Jack?' he taunted.

'No,' she admitted with a laugh. 'Not Jack.' She knew Rick was waiting for some kind of admission from her of her love for him, but she couldn't give it to him. If she were to die—and God knows she so much wanted to live now!—then it wouldn't be fair to burden him with her love. Maybe if she were to live . . . But that could still only be a possibility.

'I should have realised you were ill.' He spoke almost to himself. 'There was the night I had to break into your apartment because you'd fallen asleep, and then the excessive tiredness you felt from working, the way you sleep so heavily. I wondered if you took sleeping pills at first, but there didn't seem to be any evidence of them, so I dismissed that. I never even suspected the truth . . .!'

'You weren't supposed to,' she told him quietly. 'I wish you didn't know now.'

'Well, I'm damn glad I do!' He sat up straight, putting her firmly away from him. 'I'm not going to let you die, Shanna. You're going to live, for *me*. Do you have any idea how lucky you were to even be given the chance of an operation? My mother isn't so lucky, or you can bet she would have had it by now.'

She flushed her guilt, knowing the truth of his words. She had been a coward all this time.

'I can't understand why Henry hasn't—My God, he doesn't know, does he?' Rick breathed slowly as the colour increased in her cheeks. 'Of course he doesn't,' he spoke softly to himself. 'If he did he would never have let you strain yourself by working at *Fashion Lady*. And he would have insisted that you have surgery. You didn't tell your own brother, Shanna?' he demanded incredulously.

She turned away from the recrimination in his eyes. 'I didn't see the point of upsetting him.'

'You would rather he just found you dead one day, eh?' Rick rasped angrily. 'God, woman, you deserve a beating!' he snapped as she paled. 'Can you imagine what that would have done to Henry?'

'I didn't want to worry him . . .' she said weakly.

'Just contribute to your death by giving you a job! Hell, Shanna, if I didn't love you so much I'd beat you myself!' He stood up in forceful movements. 'Now go and get yourself dressed while I call the doctor.'

'He won't see me on a Saturday,' she shook her head as he pulled her to her feet.

'He will,' Rick said grimly. 'And if he won't then I'll find someone else who will.'

Shanna went into the bedroom to dress, feeling a certain amount of relief that Rick knew the truth, that she had been able to at last tell someone about the last six months with Perry, to explain his behaviour if not excuse it. Rick's strength had been what she had needed to go through with the operation a year ago, a strength Perry had been unable to give her despite their love for each other. When she had woken up in hospital six months ago to be told that her husband was dead, and that her own operation was urgent, she hadn't even *wanted* to live, had wanted to die.

And now—now she wanted to live, wanted to be Rick's wife, to give him the children he wanted. It had been strange the way she had never given Perry a child, despite trying for months, although the doctor had told her the body was a strange thing, that it compensated for its own weaknesses. *If* she had become pregnant, then having the baby would probably have killed her.

'He'll see us in twenty minutes,' Rick told her when she rejoined him, having dressed in casual black trousers and a bottle green blouse.

She gulped. 'He will?'

'Yes.' Rick's expression was grim.

'But——'

'I'll be right by your side all the time, Shanna,' he told her gently. 'Even if there's only a slim chance you realise we have to take it, don't you?' He held her gaze with his.

We. Yes, they were a couple now; she realised they had become so the first time she gave herself to him.

'I won't let you down, Shanna,' he told her gruffly. 'Just live for me, darling.'

She couldn't answer him, didn't speak at all on the drive to see the doctor, although her eyes widened as they drove to a residential part of London.

'I managed to find the doctor at his home.' Even Rick looked a little bashful at this intrusion. 'Once I'd explained the situation to him he said he would see us here.'

Her nervousness wasn't helped by the fact that Rick refused to leave her side even once the doctor began his examination, and she felt very conscious of his black-eyed gaze on her all the time Dr Hunt did his examination.

Finally the doctor stepped back, a tall grey-haired man in his early fifties, his casual dress pointing to this being his day off. 'You can get dressed now,' he told her. 'Well, you've reduced your chances considerably by waiting like this,' he continued bluntly. 'Although that isn't to say there's no chance,' he added hastily at Rick's groan of protest.

'How much of one is there?' Shanna asked softly, gripping Rick's hand tightly.

'Hard to say,' he frowned.

'When can you operate?' Rick demanded.

The doctor's brows rose. 'Are you a relative of Mrs Logan's?'

'Her fiancé,' he bit out arrogantly, squeezing her hand reassuringly.

Dr Hunt was frowning as he turned back to Shanna. 'But your husband . . .?'

'He died,' Rick told him tersely. 'When can you operate?' he persisted.

'That would depend——'

'On what?' Once again Rick was demanding.

'On Mrs Logan's general health at the moment, on her own will to live, and on when the operation can be scheduled.'

'Her health is fine,' Rick told him arrogantly. 'No worse than anyone else's who expects to die at any moment,' he added bitterly. 'And she'll live for me,' he stated imperiously. 'So when can you schedule the operation?'

The doctor looked disconcerted by the arrogance of this man, although he recognised a lot of it as being because of his deep love for the woman at his side. 'I——'

'Tomorrow?' Rick prompted.

'Well, no, not that soon. But——'

'How soon?' Rick's voice was taut.

'Rick, calm down,' Shanna soothed him. 'Give the doctor a chance to speak!'

He bit back his impatience with effort. 'Sorry,' he muttered to the other man.

'That's perfectly all right,' the doctor accepted. 'In your position I would feel the same way. And I agree with you that no more time should be lost. I may be able to arrange something for the end of the week——'

'Make that definite, doctor, and we'll leave you to your day off,' Rick put in eagerly.

The other man gave a resigned shrug. 'All right, the end of the week. But Mrs Logan must have complete rest until then,' he added sternly. 'And we'll want her in a couple of days before the operation for more thorough tests.

'She'll be there,' Rick told him. 'And so will I!'

It was strange, but for the last three days neither of them had talked too much about the impending operation. Oh, they calmly discussed the arrangements for her admission, and Rick drove her in himself, although Henry had wanted to come too. Her brother had had to be told, and Rick had been the one to do the telling. Henry was calm by the time he came to see Shanna, although tears glistened in his eyes. Rick had persuaded him that it would be less traumatic for her if they went to the hospital alone, and on this, her last night at home before going to hospital, Henry and Janice had brought the children over to visit for an hour, although the cheerful youngsters could have no idea of the gravity of the occasion.

And now she lay in the strength of Rick's arms, needing more than just this physical closeness, needing so much more. She began to caress his body, instantly feeling desire surge through him.

'No!' he stopped the movement of her hands.

'Sweetheart, the doctor said complete rest,' he groaned in the darkness of her bedroom.

And Rick had kept to that instruction to the letter; he had stayed with her day and night, the trip to America forgotten. Lance was despatched in his place, and Rick made sure she did nothing more strenuous than lift a cup to her lips, holding her with platonic comfort every night. 'We may never have the chance again,' she reminded him softly.

'Don't!' he choked. 'God, don't say that!' He buried his face in her hair.

Shanna could feel the heat of his tears on her cheek, and her arms tightened about him. 'Make love to me, Rick,' she requested boldly as she had once before. 'Let me go into this knowing how much you love me.'

They made love slowly, savouring each moment as if it really would have to last them a lifetime. And even when passion had been spent they remained as one, staying together like that as Shanna slept in Rick's arms, and Rick slowly, painfully, watched the black of night turn into dawn's morning light, his hold on her never wavering, as if he were willing her to live.

Shanna liked hospitals no more than Perry had, despite being in a private room, and the days passed slowly until the morning of the operation. To her surprise she woke to find Rick sitting in the chair next to her bed, his haggard expression and unshaven jaw pointing to his having been there for some time.

She frowned her concern as she sat up. 'Darling . . .?'

'If you die, Shanna,' he told her raggedly, not moving, 'you'll be killing me too.'

'No!' she cried her horror.

'Yes,' he insisted grimly. 'So you fight to live for me—and our children.'

'Rick, even after the operation—if I survive,' she

added softly, 'I won't be able to have children for some time.'

'I know that,' his eyes glittered. 'And I don't care if we have any or not. But I know they're important to you, so we will have some eventually. But not for some time—I'll want you all to myself to begin with. I'm having the ranch prepared for us, and my mother is organising the wedding for when we arrive.'

'Rick——'

'Don't think negative!' he rasped, pale beneath his dark complexion. 'I refuse to. I couldn't sleep last night,' he told her softly. 'So I did some walking instead,' he explained away his unshaven jaw. 'I saw this in a store window,' he took the ring-box out of his coat pocket, 'and I knew I had to have it for you. I had the jeweller out of bed at the crack of dawn.' He opened the box, taking out the ring and slipping it on to the third finger of her left hand. 'I want you to wear this until I can put it on your finger legally.'

It was a wedding ring, a slender gold band that fitted her finger perfectly. 'It's beautiful, Rick, but——'

'I've had it inscribed inside,' he told her huskily. 'It says "I love you, R." '

Her eyes widened. 'You made the jeweller do that this morning too? The poor man will probably never be the same again!'

'Probably,' he acknowledged unconcernedly.

'It's a beautiful ring, Rick.' She touched it lovingly. 'And thank you for the inscription. But I can't wear it during the operation.'

'You can,' he nodded. 'I already checked, and wedding rings are allowed. They put some sort of tape over it, I think.'

'But we aren't married,' she laughed.

His gaze was intent, a fire burning in the dark

depths of his eyes. 'We are in every way that matters,' he said gruffly. 'And I want some part of me with you all the time.'

Shanna swallowed convulsively. 'I'll wear the ring. Did you see the lovely flowers Cindy bought me yesterday?' she attempted to lighten the tension between them. 'How is she doing at the magazine?' she asked as he made no response to the flowers.

'Fine,' he dismissed.

'Have you been in to work at all?'

'No.' He held on tightly to the hand wearing his ring. 'I can't concentrate. I can't seem to do anything without you!'

She wanted to comfort him, to help him, but there was nothing she could do or say to make this easier for him.

A nurse came into the room at that moment, coming to a halt as she saw Rick sitting beside the bed. 'I'm afraid I'll have to ask you to leave now, Mr Dalmont,' she said briskly as she came in. 'I have to prepare Mrs Logan for theatre.'

Rick seemed to blanch, his eyes looking bloodshot and haunted. 'Could you just give us a few minutes alone? I—We won't be long.'

The nurse nodded slowly. 'A few minutes.' She gave an understanding smile before leaving.

Rick's hand tightened convulsively about Shanna's. 'Am I doing the right thing by pressurising you into this operation?' he groaned raggedly. 'Am I being selfish? Would it be better to take what time we do have and be thankful for it?'

She touched his face with loving fingers, knowing that she *could* help him—by telling the truth. 'I want more than that, Rick,' she gave him a serene smile. 'I love you, and I want to spend all my life with you, not just a few months. If anyone was being selfish it was me, by not being honest about my feelings. I thought I would save you pain, but that was wrong of me. I'll live, Rick, and it will be because we love each other, because we want a lifetime, not a short time together and then loneliness. Do you understand, darling? I'm doing this for *both of us*.'

'Shanna . . .!' His lips claimed hers in drugging intensity.

'I love you,' she clung to him fiercely. 'I love you so much.'

'That's all I needed to know.' He was smiling as he gently touched her lips with his. 'I'll be sitting right here when you wake up. And I'll be beside you for the rest of our lives.'

And he was, through all the years of their life together, as they watched their children grow up bathed in the knowledge of their parents' undying love for each other.

THE MAGIC OF JADE

When Shanna gave Alice and Steven a jade figurine for their twenty-fifth wedding anniversary, she was giving them a present fit for a Chinese emperor. Since the dawn of civilization, China has cherished jade as the most desirable of stones, a product of heaven. Fortunes were spent for tiny carved jade amulets believed to heal ills and bestow immortality.

Nephrite and jadeite are the two hard and durable minerals known as jade. Their strength is such that fifty tons of pressure is needed to crush a one-inch cube. Primitive man treasured jade tools and weapons, for unlike most stones he used, jade did not chip and edges stayed razor sharp. Artisans through the ages have revered jade for its beauty. In Confucius's day, pure white, blue or the radiant green stones, found in Burma and the mountains of central Asia, were laboriously worked by carvers into ornamental dragons that were thought to ward off evil or fish-shaped "soundstones" that emitted a clear musical tone when struck.

In the Americas, the ancient Aztecs drank a mixture of jade powder and water to prevent kidney disease. Spanish conquerors took Mexican jade carvings to Europe, and *piedra de ijada,* or "stone of the loins," became *le jade* in French. Today jade is found in such diverse places as Poland, New Zealand and British Columbia.

The centuries-old treadle lathe is still the Chinese lapidary's most valued tool. With the aid of fine abrasives, jade is ground and turned into smooth curvaceous figurines. It could be said that the craftsman, who works with precision and care at his ageless art, employs the same delicate balance needed for lasting romance!